Shadows: A Love Story

(With a novella 'Lingering Pain')

Niranjan Tasneem

DIAMOND BOOKS

ISBN : 978-81-288-3041-9

© Author

Published by
Diamond Pocket Books Pvt. Ltd.
X-30, Okhla Industrial Area, Phase-II
New Delhi-110020
Phone : 011-40712200
E-mail : sales@dpb.in
Website : www.diamondbook.in

Shadows: A Love Story
Niranjan Tasneem

*Dedicated to the memory of
my pleasant stay in Shimla
for a decade from October, 1951
to October, 1961*

Foreword

During my stay in Shimla for a decade, I noticed the emergence of the New Woman. For long, in a sort of captivity, woman had suffered a lot. The freedom of the land changed the social as well as political scenario. In the new set-up woman's quest for her identity brought her in conflict with the familial and social prejudices. She wanted to play her role as an individual and not merely as a daughter, a wife and a mother. Her creative energies sought release from 'human bondage' so as to play her role as a liberated human being.

Shadows is a love story with a difference. The lovers fall in love at first sight but they reserve their options for the life to come. They want to understand each other, to fathom the depth of their love for each other and to ensure dignified attitude for each other. There is a dilemma in the boy's mind whether it is obligatory to marry the girl one loves. Like John Keats he wants to perpetuate the sublime feeling of love without lowering it to the mundane level– *'For ever wilt thou love, and she be fair !'* On the other hand, for the girl, love is her whole existence. She is in agony when the lover dithers on one pretext or the other. Later, when she marries someone else, she liberates herself from the past and turns a new leaf in her life. What she considered her destination turns out to be a milestone in her life– "Do you mean I should light a lamp on the grave of my love lost and sit beside it to keep its flame alight with the oil of my tears? No, I could not do that. My love is alive and it will never die."

Lingering Pain is a story of passion. In it, the situation is entirely different. A married woman wants space for her personality to develop. She hates being regarded merely as an object for sexual gratification. Her mind craves for romantic response to her tender feelings. Romantic view of life is not an escape from the realities of life but a prelude to seeking a glimpse of the joy of life. Otherwise, the body tends to slip into an abyss of nothingness– "Rama felt a strong tremor in her body. She felt as if she were shrinking and had turned into a dot. The dot began to dance before her eyes– a savage dance. She shut her eyes for a moment. Suddenly a hand turned into a snake and moved sideways over her, its venom permeated every pour of her body and her limbs became listless."

The readers may find in these fictional works two dominant images of life which are–

'Like Juno's swans

still-coupled and inseparable.'

–Niranjan Tasneem (Prof)
77, Vishal Nagar Extn.,
Ludhiana— 141 013
0161-2564277
Email : gursheen@sify.com

Preface

Shadows is pre-eminently a love story, laid in sylvan setting of a convent school and its cluster of teachers' houses. The surroundings are pastoral with nature rich in pine, cedar, rhododendrons and flowers such as roses, sweet-peas and dahlias. The story is unfolded lyrically in a series of brief flashbacks. Raminder meets Jasbir, who is with her husband and child, after five years, while travelling in a train compartment. The train is moving forward but the minds of the lovers go back to the happenings of the years past. After each flashback one returns to the train compartment where Raminder and Jasbir are engaged in processing the loose ends in their love relationship. The technique of continual withdrawing from the present to the past, interspersed with interior monologues in the stream of consciousness vein, is natural not laboured. In my view the Indian novelists should use this technique to enrich their narrative repertoire.

In addition to this significant dimension of his narrative craft, Tasneem uses a body of illusion from English literature. To illustrate this dimension of his fictional craft, it is worthwhile pointing out that in dealing with Raminder's relationship with Jasbir, he sees her as being more beautiful than Helen and Cleopatra. Once in the room in his cottage, alone, Raminder slips into depression, into 'the depth of a well.' He, however, returns to his sane self after the encounter with depression.

So far we have dealt with Jasbir and Raminder's love relationship in terms of narrative skeletally. But **Shadows** also propounds a view of what love is all about. Both Raminder and Jasbir go through an alchemy process which is articulated in their conversations and exchanges of letters and their actions. For Jasbir, love is consciousness – a thrill, enflaming, burning, parching, but it must embrace the body. No wonder before leaving the Jutog school she takes the initiative of consummating her love with Raminder–

"He huddled near her. For a while they were silent and then his fingers went into the soft flesh of her arm. Jasbir's gaze shifted from the calendar to the fingers on her arm. Then she looked at Raminder and saw a desire, a pleading and a pain in the contours of his face. At once she felt very weak and utterly helpless..... The whole atmosphere got enveloped in a grey mist. The sea waves kept striking against a rock, the flame of the lamp flickered in the wind and then– a firework burst in the air and countless tiny stars went flying all around."

Though Raminder and Jasbir's relationship remains in the focus throughout the **Shadows,** what makes the novel a depth exploration, though in the lyrical vein, on love in the presence of other love relationships. One such relationship is that between Amarjit and Raminder. Amarjit loves her teacher ardently. She is spunky, hangs around in the vicinity when Raminder and Jasbir are together. In the school picnic to Glen, she confronts Raminder when the latter is alone and enacts her love for him boldly. As if that were not enough, she slips a letter declaring her love for him in a blue envelope in her copybook for which she is scolded. In the brief encounter following this dare, she is scolded by Raminder who behaves like a puritan prig.

To encapsulate! Tasneem as a novelist is *Sahaj* into *Bhava* grasp, is reflective without being ideological. Not being ideological he is unaffiliated to any school or group. He is into nature, having absorbed Shimla for ten years. He absorbed it exhilaratingly having come from crowded, dingy Amritsar streets. The mountainscopy was liberating. He experienced a prolonged unknown Mode of Being which inseminated him for good. In all his novels, such as **Glittering Sands, The Dawn of Freedom** and **The Lost Meaning,** he invokes Nature impressionistically. On the other hand, he represents states of his protagonist's consciousness expressionistically to bring out the difficult symbology of the soul.

–(Dr) Som P. Ranchan

Former Head,
Department of English
Himachal Pradesh University,
Shimla.

*Man's love is of man's life a thing apart;
'Tis woman's whole existence.*
— *Lord Byron*

1

Raminder entered a first class compartment and looked around. A pair of dark eyes mesmerised him. Her whole being was undulating as if in the wide, limitless ocean of moonlight. He wanted to talk to her but could think of nothing. Five years back they had been so close, with their hearts beating in unison. And today? There was a big gulf between them, though physically they were so near at that time.

Before he could regain his composure and say something, a man entered the compartment, followed by a bearer with a tea-tray. He was, in all probability, her husband. She said something to him and he invited Raminder to join them for tea–

"Thanks, but I have already ordered mine",

"Never mind, we'll share that with you", she said in a soft tone.

The voice had the melodious notes of the days gone by and the fragrance of the memories still cherished. He felt incapable of refusing. Going over to join them, he noticed a child of about three or four years, sleeping by the woman's side. 'This child could have been his own'–the bitterness of this idea had a toxic effect on his very being. The sensation of an electric shock ran through his spine. He stole a glance at the woman.......... her long eyelashes fanned her rosy cheeks.

She started making tea. While doing so she automatically added a little above one tea-spoon of sugar to his cup. A smile lit up the corners of his eyes. His gaze arrested hers and a flash of light appeared and vanished as quickly, just as a shaft of lightning lights up the dark horizon for a moment and then disappears. Meanwhile, her husband, quite unaware of the current in the atmosphere, was covering the child with a blanket.

❑

2

Raminder had been in the Oak View Annexe for about three months when Jasbir stepped in one evening. After coming back from the Convent, he had just changed and switched on the kettle. When he heard a faint knock at the door, he opened it to find Jasbir there–

"You, here?"

"May I?"

"You don't have to ask. The place is your own."

"Mine? But how..........?"

"Oh ! I said it just by the way. Hope you didn't take it ill."

"It's better not to, under these circumstances."

"What circumstances, by the way?"

"Well..........er..........look, the kettle is boiling. Lest you should take ill of something and I am not offered even a cup of tea."

"Not at all. Please sit down while I prepare tea."

"Nothing doing ! I shall prepare tea. Just tell me where can I find tea-leaves, milk and sugar?"

"One thing at a time, please. Tea-leaves, I couldn't find in the morning. Perhaps you'll get them somewhere around if you try. Meanwhile, I'll rinse these cups once again."

Raminder took two cups and two saucers to the bathroom. The taps were dry but there was water in the bath tub. He put some soap on the cups and saucers, dipped them in the tub and went back to the room. By this time Jasbir had laid tea but she looked very annoyed about something. Raminder was surprised at the change in her within the last couple of minutes. He remained nonchalant for a while. Jasbir made a cup and gave it to him. He was lost in his thoughts and it was only after he had started taking his tea when he realised that Jasbir had not made herself a cup.

"Why don't have you some?" She kept silent as if she had not heard him. When Raminder began to pour it into her cup, she checked him, "No, I don't want any tea."

"What will you have then? Coffee or..........?"

"Yes, come on, what else can you offer me?"

"Coffee, chocolate or cocoa or.........."

"Nothing else?"

"What else?"

"What's there in the closet?"

"Oh, that ! That.......... "Raminder took a long sip and continued–

"You know, a friend of mine was here, sometime back; the one who writes Urdu poetry. And, Urdu poets always manage a round, wherever they are."

"But how on earth can one person consume all these bottles? You must also have."

"Oh, you don't know him. He takes three bottles of beer at a go and doesn't mind whisky in addition."

Shadows: A Love Story

"But how awful! Why do you have friendship with such persons? I really detest this..........?"

"Anyway, he was all praise for you."

"For me? How?"

"Paid you compliments."

"Come off it, I know you are kidding now."

"No kidding, swear. He also said that you have a Mona Lisan smile."

"Mona Lisan? Oh! I just don't know how people get all these funny ideas into their heads."

"Well, he at least is right."

"But when did he see me?"

"He came to look me up in the Convent once. We both went into the library while you, with some other teachers, were sitting outside in the sun, at a little distance."

"So, you watch people surreptitiously!"

"I wanted him to meet you but he was a bit reluctant due to his shyness."

"Alright, forget it, will you promise me something?"

"What's that?"

"That you will never drink again."

"But why should I make such promise? As it is, life is already full of restraints."

"Only the savage lead irresponsible life."

"And I have not risen above that level, yet. The truth, actually, lies only in savagery. All else is pretence or delusion."

"Then there is no such thing as civilization?"

"There is but that's only a dark veil over reality, just a decor."

"What's the need of this veil or decor, as you say?"

"Yes, that's precisely what I say; why go after it?"

She became silent and he was lost in a reverie about the narrow-minded approach of the middle-class girls who must argue about the good and the bad in every little thing, when nothing in itself is either good or bad. It is one's approach to it that makes it so. How about the naked body of a woman? Is that, in itself, good or bad? The great artists of Ajanta and Elora have depicted women almost naked, the statues of Khajuraho are not only nude but are also locked in erotic embrace. Liquor can be condemned because it causes physical ailments and economic defluxion, but, at the same time, its potential as a medium for relieving man of stresses and strains, even though temporarily, cannot be denied. It helps him transcend time and space, while it makes him capable of impersonal thinking at the same time. Wine is not, of course, the only source of intoxication; it is there in meditation or in the eyes of the beloved. But our Bourgeoisie–Raminder kept on thinking–they are all idolaters. They make idols out of hackneyed, worn-out ideals, to put them on a pedestal and worship them.

"I really like Mrs. Nixon's approach to life," he said, looking deep into Jasbir's eyes.

"What's that?" Jasbir felt flummoxed.

"She has not cowered under the weight of sufferings and sorrows but has made these the foundation of the structure of her life."

"But she should have had no contact with another man, after Mr. Nixon's death."

"Why not?"

"Love, I think, is an infinite feeling and not just the flitting shadow of a stray cloud."

"Love should never be allowed to stand in the way of the development of one's personality."

"But Mrs. Nixon's relations with Master Sharavat after Mr. Nixon.........."

"This relationship is the evidence of her love for life.........."

"But isn't it a disgrace to her love for Mr. Nixon?"

"Love for him and its memory have now become an integral part of Mrs. Nixon's psyche–apart from it, nothing else exists."

A few months back when he had joined Loreto Convent, as Tutor of English, he was deeply impressed by Jasbir's personality. She was like a black buck, mad after its own musky fragrance. All this had a strange impact on him. Why did she impress him so much? He had known more beautiful and much smarter girls but none of them had made an indelible mark on the screen of his mind. When he went to join the second year of his M.A. in English at Chandigarh, he had come in contact with a girl who proved to him that a modern girl could surpass even Helen or Cleopatra, if she wanted to. For her, he had fought many battles of Troy and Nile. In return he got his heart pierced through sharp arrows. He had got himself bitten by her cobras as well as asps and the poison had seeped into his being. But all this hullabaloo had been incapable of gratifying the yearnings of his parched soul.

That day when he saw Jasbir for the first time he felt as if a lively bird had come to perch on a dry twig, making it bloom suddenly. The staff of the Convent consisted of some dozen mistresses and a couple of masters. The place had the atmosphere of Thomas Hardy's novel *"Tess."* Raminder felt just as Angel Clare had done when he went to learn dairy farming in that romantic set-up. Only *Tess*, of all the milk-maids on the farm, could tingle and stimulate his superfine sensibilities.

The elegant building of the Loreto Convent could be seen on the Jutog hill, some seven miles from Shimla. At a small slope along the Jutog railway station was the Tu-Tu Bazaar and where it ended, the road circumvented along the high hill. That road led to the Jutog hill across a small bridge. A little farther from the Bridge was a crossing from which three different paths emerged. The one, on the right, led to the army officers' residences situated on a small hillock. On the left, beyond a big orchard, was the Convent surrounded by pine and cedar trees. The opposite path went through the Jutog market and ended at a bypass, from which the path on the right led to the village Arki, situated in a valley, a little below. Towards the left, a track sloped to the European graveyard. There were about twenty graves there–graves of some army officers, their wives and children whom Death had taken unawares in a foreign land. Wild-rose creepers had clung to the marble platforms surrounded by a dense-growth of trees.

On the first day of his joining, Raminder went around the building of the Convent. Three small blocks had been constructed on the three sides of a beautiful lawn, where Roses, Dahlias, Cosmos, Sweet Peas and Narcissi tossed 'their heads in a sprightly dance.' Tall pines stood majestically erect there. On the left side was a tennis-court screened by a wiremesh wall. Beyond the court was a deep abyss through which a monsoon streamlet roared during the rainy season. In winter this abyss turned into a big lake, covered with a milk-white sheet of snow. To the left of the Convent was a wide track that went through a growth of apples, walnuts and pears, ending at Principal Mrs. Singh's residence. Across it was the Oak View Cottage, where the staff of the Convent lived in separate suites. Farther on, on a slight slope, stood the Oak View Annexe.

On his first round of the Convent, he came to an abrupt halt in front of the Junior Cambridge class. He had no idea that Jasbir was taking the class. In the class-room, about twenty five girls were scribbling something in their notebooks. They

Shadows: A Love Story

were intent on their work when he walked in. He saw, rather felt, a movement in the window on the right side and before he could be aware of the situation, he was face to face with a full bosom, a little tilted up nose and black dreamy eyes.

"Do come in———."

"Oh! I didn't know you were here. You are writing something, perhaps."

"I was trying to."

"Verses or a short-story?"

"No, I intended to write something concerning criticism."

"That's a pretty serious thing, I must say."

"Actually, I'm appearing for M.A. in English this year."

"That's good."

"Won't you sit down?"

"Thanks, but I have a class right now."

"But in the next period, we'll have recess." Raminder felt cornered.

During the break he met some other teachers also. Mrs. Singh too came to join them in the refreshment room. Meeting them was a pleasure. Coffee was getting cold but their conversation had gained warmth. Jasbir was sitting with a couple of other teachers and their cups were lying on the window-sill close by. She was gazing out of the window but her ears were attuned to his conversation with someone. He himself was looking at her, though listening to Mrs. Singh who was explaining the Senior Cambridge syllabus to him.

❏

3

The train was moving very fast and they were the only four occupants of the compartment. Her husband was asleep and his snoring was audible above the noise and rattle of the train. All the lights except a bulb had been switched off. Raminder was lying on his back with his eyes focused on the roof. At times he glanced at the girl who would already be looking at him. When their eyes met for the flash of a second, they averted them at once.

The girl was fumbling about the leaves of a pictorial magazine for the umpteenth time. Her legs were covered with a part of the blanket, the half of which was covering the child. The child was fast asleep, totally unaware of his surroundings. The train caused quite a tremor when it changed track. The magazine fell from the girl's hands. Raminder tried, not in reality but in imagination, to pick it up and give it back to her. Instead of picking up the magazine, she kept gazing at him, as if in a trance. He took the initiative–

"Jasbir!"

"Yes........?" A pebble dropped in the still waters and created ripples which appeared for a while on the surface and then disappeared.

"Are you regretting something?"

"No.........." But then there was a whirlpool which went deeper and deeper.

"Then, what makes you unhappy?"

"I am unhappy, not for myself, but for you."

"For me?"

"Yes, you had to suffer so much because of me."

"How absurd!" said Raminder who considered it wrong to weigh love in the scales of sufferings. In a more emphatic tone, he blurted out, "I have not suffered due to anyone."

"Don't be dishonest to yourself, please. Why did you leave your residence in the Convent after I had gone away and why did you leave afterwards the place itself? Didn't you tell Mrs. Nixon that you could not live there any longer and that you hated the place?"

"Do you remember you told Miss Ranchan, on your wedding, that you were mine and only mine, once and for all, no matter where you were."

"I did say that——"

"Wasn't it a vain effort to console yourself and didn't it amount to self-deception?"

"Let's not go into details, now. Tell me, why haven't you married yet?"

"Because you have. Isn't that enough?"

"Why not; It's enough, more than enough!"

Jasbir quietly gazed out of the window, perhaps in an attempt to hide the tears welling up in her eyes. Raminder resumed staring vacantly at the ceiling. It was all quiet in the compartment except her husband's snoring which could not be submerged even in the rattle of the running train. In spite of all these sounds, the compartment seemed to be an island where deep silence prevailed.

❑

4

Mrs. Nixon was an attractive woman of about thirty five. Born in a Hindu Khanna family she had married an Anglo-Indian, Mr. Nixon, an orchestra composer in a reputed Lahore restaurant. She was Montessori-trained and had been teaching in a Public School before marriage. After she got married, she gave up that job. Those were the colourful days of her life, full of gaiety and felicity. So carried away was she by the flood of emotions that she did not even realise when Mr. Nixon crossed the limit of drinking for pleasure and turned into an alcoholic. What used to create pleasant sensations started excavating his body from within. Just before the Partition, Mr. Nixon fell a victim to consumption and his condition went on deteriorating with the passage of time. They shifted from Lahore to Delhi and the circle of their acquaintances dwindled. Mr. Nixon was in no state to work for living and they had no means to fall back upon. Finding no way-out, Mrs. Nixon took up a job in a school. Though they just managed to survive on her salary, medical care was always a problem. In spite of many odds in her way, she fought against disease and hunger for as long as seven years, but Mr. Nixon could not recover. When he died, she got so depressed that she left Delhi to find recluse at this hill-station. Then, unknown to anyone, she herself took to drinking–perhaps as an endeavour to forget herself. After

Shadows: A Love Story

that Master Sharavat came to live with her in her suite in the Oak Cottage. Their relationship had no name of any sort.

Sitting with Mrs. Nixon and talking to her for long hours gave Raminder a peculiar pleasure and, at that time, a feeling of happy tranquility descended upon him. She spoke English with correct accent and he wanted to drink deep in the rippling fountain of her words. He often spent his evenings with her in her cosy resort. Sharavat, no doubt, had an air of hypocrisy and pretence about himself but basically he was like an innocent child. His life was an enigma. He was carrying on his love affair with Miss Ranchan, a mistress at the Convent, and was living with Mrs. Nixon in the same room.

"Raminder, I found Jasbir in a very dejected mood today. What is the matter?" Mrs. Nixon asked Raminder one evening.

"Shall I tell you, Mrs. Nixon?" Sharavat interrupted, "while teaching her Greek Poetic Drama, he got annoyed with her and called her silly. She was so hurt that she started crying."

"He is fibbing, Mrs. Nixon", Raminder said, while sipping his whisky, "I have not been teaching her for quite sometime."

"Then there must be something else." Mrs. Nixon at that time looked younger by ten years.

"Nothing much. When you come to know, you'll only laugh at it. I just told her that she was putting on weight and asked her to give me a tip or two on the subject for improving my lean structure. At this she started shedding tears."

"You can't call her plump; she is just reasonably........."

"No, Mrs. Nixon–a woman can be seen only through a man's eyes."

"Man can fall at times for a mole on the cheek, ignoring the rest of the structure."

"In fact, it's a matter of something pricking the heart, needle like."

"Now I get it", Sharavat jumped in, "Jasbir has a sharp nose, of course not needle like."

"And Miss Ranchan a sharp tongue." A smile played in the corners of Raminder's eyes and Sharavat murmured with a sigh,

"She is different, my dear Rammi, she is altogether different."

"Look at him Mrs. Nixon, he is sighing like a furnace."

"She is a very homely type of a girl and he is merely wasting his time." Mrs. Nixon at once became thoughtful.

"Mrs. Nixon, I am not joking, I just cannot live without her." Sharavat tried not to meet her gaze.

"I hate sentimental people." Raminder took the last pull at his drink and put the empty glass on the table.

"And who is not sentimental? There can, of course, be the difference of degree." Sharavat fixed his gaze on Raminder's face.

"That is the main difference, Sharavat." Raminder was deeply convinced of the truth of his statement.

It was Christmas Eve. They had already drained a bottle. The room was getting too warm and Mrs. Nixon took off her gown. Her face expressed deep peace and contentment and there was rhythm in every movement of hers. Time had stopped in a valley and life had drifted into a deep and dark wood. Once again Raminder glued his gaze on her face. He suddenly realised that she was a modern woman who had got everything but still lacked something. Smouldered by the fires of life, modern woman was no longer a cure for man's woes, rather she was herself in dire need of something drastic to relieve her of the lingering pain within her. Then he thought of Jasbir who had the self-confidence of a healthy animal. She was aware of her requirements and conscious of her shortcomings. She had

Shadows: A Love Story

a fervent desire to see her hopes fulfilled. She was confined to her environment but was always on the alert to guard her reputation. She did not want to go beyond the set rules of society. What a helpless being man is, thought Raminder, who cannot rise much above his surroundings! How could he in personal capacity break the shackles of the society? What mattered ultimately was not whether an objective had been attained or not; it was the effort made for that purpose which was important–a complete whole hearted effort.

Mrs. Nixon looked extremely graceful and elegant but in comparison to her, Sharavat appeared puny and ignoble. He was like a helpless babe who only knew what hunger was and where milk could be had. Beyond that he was totally inconsequential and absolutely weak. Raminder could discern a desire, a pain in his eyes. He was like an illegitimate child to Mrs. Nixon, a responsibility that she had to carry. She had found a child, wrapped up in the rag of humiliation, lying on a heap of rubbish. Mrs. Nixon had absorbed someone's stain in her soul and in return gave the offspring the warmth of motherly love. When this child became stubborn or did not listen to her or was annoyed with her, she kept quiet and did not upbraid him. At such times, her heart brimmed over with affection and pity for him.

❑

5

"Sir, please come over to our place tomorrow evening, it's my birthday." Amarjit, a senior Cambridge student, gave him a card. Raminder looked at her:

"Haven't you forgotten your childhood, yet?"

"Sir, my parents are celebrating my birthday, not I."

"Yes, children celebrate their own birthdays while grown ups need their parents to do so."

"Yes, Sir......." Soon she realised that she had fallen into the trap. "Sorry Sir, as a matter of fact, every year we.........."

"O.K. Have you invited anyone else from here?"

"No one as yet. I shall perhaps ask Mrs. Singh and if you wish, Miss Jasbir.........."

"No, no, why should I? On my part I shall try to make it."

"Sir, please do come."

"All right."

What a sweet kid, he thought. He had often felt that she had a deep regard for him. Perhaps she considered him a good teacher and an ideal person. This satisfied his ego. Raminder had often talked to her but the small conversation he had with her that day had caused a turmoil in his heart. He was touched by her sweetness, her elegance and her likeness to a blossoming lily– erect yet delicate. All this had filled him

Shadows: A Love Story

with an urge to take her in his arms, to kiss her, to feel the dewdrops of her voice fall on his face and to inhale them with his breath. Would that she were his own, very own !

The next day, he reached there. Not many people had been invited. Except Mrs. Singh, there was nobody else from the Convent. He wished he had not come, for how could he mix up with army officers and their wives, with their different ways of thinking and different views of life? But he was mistaken. Underneath the surface of formality and politeness, they were all alike–beads of the same string. There was only the difference of mental censor and when that was lifted, they were all the same. He too got up when the menfolk, having finished the boring affair of taking tea with ladies, went into the bar-room.

He was a little reticent at first. How could he drink with those Majors and Colonels who were fathers of the children he taught at the school? They might take a bad view of it and entertain the notion that the education of their children was in wrong hands. But no, those people did not deny him a little pleasure just because he was a teacher. He was also a human being for them, a normal human being with all his weaknesses.

Shortly afterwards a car came to a stop outside and Major Grewal went to receive his guests. With him came a gentleman whom Raminder at once recognised as the Company Commandant.

They exchanged pleasantries and Raminder was surprised to see that the Company Commandant had recognised him at once. There was unmistakable warmth in his hand-shake. Raminder recollected his first meeting with him. Some months ago, he was busy in a game with the girls of his senior class. In the game a girl whispered something in his ear and ran. Others came in rapid succession. In a hurry, the girls either fell on him or their lips brushed against his neck just below his ears. He was quite oblivious of the fact that someone had been watching him from a distance. Before long a call came for him from Mrs. Singh. It surprised him as she never called any member of her staff during the games period.

In Mrs. Singh's office he was introduced to an army officer who nodded stiffly in answer to his greeting. Raminder felt small but then, he conceded in his mind that an army officer had to keep his dignity, though it appeared a little out of place at that time:

"Raminder, don't you think that a lady teacher is better suited for this sort of a game?" Mrs. Singh's tone was a bit apologetic.

"I see no harm in the present arrangement." Raminder fixed his gaze on the officer.

"But I do. I don't much like the idea of our young girls coming in such a close contact with a man."

"But why do you take it in that light? Here we maintain a purely teacher-taught relationship." Raminder was finding it hard to keep his temper in control.

Mrs. Singh got nervous as the talk had taken quite an unexpected turn. She knew Raminder and was familiar with his views and attitudes. This was in a way an allegation on him and the ultimate responsibility came down to her. On his part, Raminder had no idea that the officer concerned was the chairman of the school council. The problem, however, was not personal but concerned a principle.

They kept on arguing for fifteen or twenty minutes. Raminder soon found out that he had an adamant fanatic to deal with. Talking still they both came out and Mrs. Singh followed them. Slowly they reached the gate where his car had been parked. The chauffeur opened the rear door for the Commandant. He shook hands with Raminder and pulled him a little closer–

"Anyway, Master Raminder, if you were in my place you would have said what I have. At the same time I don't deny that in your case. I would have said the same as you did– still, how I wish I were in your place!" They both smiled in complete understanding of each other. But the smile on Mrs. Singh's face was enigmatic.

Now, once again, he was face to face with that commandant who was surprised to see him without his glass. He drew Major Grewal's attention to it. When he learnt that Raminder had refused to drink, he frowned at him:

"Why don't you drink, youngman?"

"I don't feel like, Sir."

"What non-sense! To hell with such inhibitions." A guffaw rang in the room and Raminder was laughing the loudest.

The next day, Jasbir was angry with him but he knew not why. A little later when he noticed a glint in Mrs. Singh's eyes, it did not take him long to understand. Just to nettle Jasbir, Mrs. Singh had advertised in the morning that Raminder was there at Amarjit's party the previous evening. Jasbir was jealous of Amarjit. She had a feeling that Amarjit spied on her, for whenever she stood talking to Raminder, the latter made it a point to come and stand by them on one pretext or another.

Raminder was not surprised to note that Mrs. Singh had advertised Raminder's presence in the birthday party. She wanted Jasbir to be cross with him and whenever they were cross with each other, Mrs. Singh derived a strange kind of pleasure from it. On such occasions she went out of her way to be nice to him, called him to her office, talked to him, laughed with him and served him coffee. Very romantically she would then ask–

"Have you ever loved anyone or only others go on breaking their hearts over you?"

This made him blush and he pretended to concentrate on stirring sugar in his coffee.

Raminder made no effort to talk to Jasbir that day. He was loath even to look at her. Such behaviour and such hypocrisy antagonised him. He hated people being so touchy over trifles. He refused to be regarded as the sole property of someone, just as he never wanted to make anyone his own possession.

Whenever Jasbir was annoyed thus, he felt something shrink within him, as if an ocean were drying up into a lake. He considered all this humbug futile and hypocritical. He knew that jealousy was the main evidence of love but he did not accept it as natural; it was a drawback, a shortcoming. His feelings for Jasbir were not stable. At times his heart overflowed with love for her and he was ready to do anything for her but, at some other time, she repelled him and he wanted to have no relation, whatsoever, with her. He often wondered why the feelings of love and hatred had got so intermingled in his mind. The same emotion, that evoked love in him, later turned into dislike. Sometimes Jasbir appeared to him as a total stranger but the very next day he felt her presence pulsate in every beat of his heart.

Later, when her mental horizon was swept of all dark clouds, Jasbir stormed upon him in the library. He was sitting in a corner, reading a book. She put her hand on his eyes and as she bent over him, he felt the warm pressure of her breasts on his shoulders. All his irritation vanished at this touch. He put his arm round her waist and pulled her to him but she quickly disentangled herself and settled on the sofa beside him:

Shadows: A Love Story

"I know you don't love me at all."

"Like hell you know! My love for you vibrates in every fibre of my being."

"And to which play does this dialogue belong?"

"Aren't we enacting one ourselves?"

"How? This is a fact, a reality, Raminder."

"But for others it amounts to nothing short of a dramatic sequence– Mrs. Singh, for example."

"Don't mention Mrs. Singh. She just cannot bear to see us happy, even for a moment."

"But, Jasbir, what would happen if she sees us closeted in this corner, behind these almirahs?"

Jasbir did not say anything. She only blushed and cast her glance downward. He saw the wild roses bloom in her cheeks. At this something happened somewhere, perhaps in the deep recesses of his heart, and a tremor ran through his spine. When she held his gaze, she could not stand its intensity. Flustered, she suddenly remembered something to be done. Raminder stared at her retreating figure; her saree did nothing to conceal her curves.

That evening, at six, he went over to Jasbir's. He did not like doing so, but could not hold himself back, either. Her Papa was at home. He was a manager to some army contractor and had been residing there for the past ten years or so. This meeting, as it progressed, depressed Raminder and the ageing gentleman too did not seem to be much pleased about it either:

"Hello! How do you happen to be here?" He outrightly asked Raminder. He could think of no answer. Sensing his embarrassments, the Papa continued, "You also teach in the Convent with Jasbir? My wife mentioned once. We saw you in the market the other day; Mrs. Nixon was with you."

"Yes, we often go out together. That day, perhaps, we were returning home from Shimla after viewing an English movie."

"Master Sharavat was not with you."

"He didn't go with us, that day."

"What exactly is the relationship between these two? It's too bad....."

Raminder's glance was settled on his face for some time. Then he came out with a calculated retort, "I have not yet made up my mind about what is good and what is bad. Moreover, it varies from person to person. What is bad for you may be quite in order for me; I might like it, as well."

"You come of a good family, I presume", he carried on, "but your mixing up with such people....."

Raminder remained nonchalant and put a little more sugar in his tea. He sipped his tea with a little sound and then pursed his lips. The Papa, however, continued, "you should not cultivate such people." On hearing this, Jasbir turned back from the door; her face had lost colour.

❏

6

The train stopped at a station for two or three minutes and then moved on again. Jasbir had her eyes closed, perhaps she was asleep. She had placed both her hands, palms downwards, on the magazine lying on her breast. The child awoke once and then went back to sleep. Her husband turned on his side and stopped snoring. Raminder lifted up the shutter and peered out into the dark, but could see nothing. The pale, lifeless slice of the moon had hidden itself behind the trees on the distant hill. Even then its light sieved through the leaves:

"Don't you feel cold with that window open?" Jasbir stretched herself fully and pulled up the blanket over her.

"I thought you were asleep." He put the shutter down.

"No, I was thinking."

"Of what?"

"That you never really loved me."

"How can you say that? What were our struggles for, if not for love? Whatsoever, it made us almost mad?"

"It was all my fault. I forced myself on you, became a burden for you and you, on your part, didn't want to show any weakness on this count."

"No, no, no!!! It wasn't that. I loved you, loved you tremendously and hopelessly."

"But when? You never expressed it fully till those last few days, when it was too late."

"Earlier I didn't know, had no faith."

"Faith in whom? Me? My love?"

"No", Raminder paused for a moment, "no, not you." His voice then emerged as if out of a deep well, "But I didn't know for sure whether I loved you or not. No, it wasn't even that. I certainly and positively loved you but I did not know, at the same time, how essential it was for us to be married, to be married at all."

"For quite some time you were a puzzle to me, I could not understand you. I had no idea what lay in the depths of your heart and I didn't want to be humiliated by disclosing what was in mine."

"When the subject of your marriage came up, I felt as if I were being deprived of something very dear and precious to me. I could hardly bear to see you go to someone else, but till then I had never discovered the intensity of my own passion, the depth of my own love."

"But when I left, why did you behave as if you were mentally deranged or something? Why did you lose touch with everyone? Then, you too left that place–I have missed no details about you."

"That was a phase, a condition, a situation." Raminder leaned against the window and closed his eyes. Time had gained speed while the pulse of life was faltering and the heartbeats were feeble.

❑

Shadows: A Love Story

7

"You look like Jesus Christ today." Mrs. Nixon's gaze was fixed on Raminder's face.

"How's that, Mrs. Nixon?" he asked, slightly taken aback.

"Your soft, fine hair, small full beard and the slim muscular body......" Mrs. Nixon looked at him from head to feet in a manner that made him blush. He felt like a new bride that must blush, with secret pleasure though, when her husband admired her for her beauty. That was the first time Raminder had come before her directly after washing his long hair, that covered his neck on three sides, while his beard had also been loosened. The comparison with Christ pleased him, but he had forgotten that the sufferings Christ underwent could not be segregated from his sinewy body:

"You know, Mrs. Singh was furious with Jasbir yesterday."

"Yes, I know she gets annoyed with her for nothing."

"She believes that Jasbir writes letters in the class."

"But that's absolute nonsense! She does no such thing. I scribble something in a notebook and send it to her in the morning. Later she puts down her ideas in it at home and returns it to me the next day."

"Then she must have seen you doing that."

"No, Mrs. Nixon. Someone has poisoned her ears, that's about all."

"Who could have done that?"

"I suspect Sharavat," Raminder got serious, "A few days back I told him that, to avoid Mrs. Singh's disapproval, we did not meet in the campus but expressed our feelings in writing. I had also mentioned the notebook in that connection."

"Can't say," Mrs. Nixon replied in a small voice, "he is out of his element these days."

"Whatever for?"

"Miss Ranchan has stopped paying him attention and he goes rattling her name, day in and day out. Says he'd either marry her or commit suicide."

"How preposterous! Sheer nonsense!!" Raminder tied his hair up and wrapped the gown round himself fully.

"Listen, your play was a great success," said Mrs. Nixon, switching on the tea kettle.

"Whose role did you like the most?"

"Everyone liked Amarjit's. She could not be recognized when she appeared as a lawyer in a steel grey suit–it was yours, wasn't it?"

"Yes, and it suited her."

"She is like you–thin and delicate."

"Mrs. Nixon, I am not that thin but whenever I go home my mother grumbles that I have lost weight."

"She is right, also. You were much healthier when you came here first."

"But I feel much better now."

"Yes, you must be feeling on top of the world. Someone has said–'The more colour you lose, the fairer you look.' Isn't it?"

He made no reply but took his cup of coffee from Mrs. Nixon. He thought that Mrs. Nixon must also have once loved

Shadows: A Love Story

and been carried away by the current of her feelings. Perhaps she had to suffer a lot and was upset for long. She looked sad, weary and listless as if she were sitting on the shore, counting the waves and watching the swimmers. The important thing was that she had not surrendered herself to the vicissitudes of life to deal with her as they pleased. Her mind was still vibrant.

He felt an urge to hold her by her slim, fair arm and asked, "Mrs. Nixon, I am like a shell lying on the sands of the Blue Ocean. I have no purpose in life. Touch me with your lips, please. And breathe life into me. Or bring forth the most poisonous snake from under your bed, O' my Cleopatra, and let its poison run though my veins."

Mrs. Nixon got up from her place, curtained the windows and switched on the light. Then settling down near him, she said, "You are passing through a very difficult phase these days."

"How can you say that, Mrs. Nixon?"

"Your lifestyle reveals it. She has fully captured your head and heart, isn't it?"

"All I know is that I am in the grip of my own feelings and emotions."

"But someone does inspire you. Isn't it?"

"No, I feel I have not yet met anyone who could inspire me; if I have, I haven't realised it. When I could not find my icon in someone, I moulded it to the likeness of an imaginary person. But to tell you the truth, the shape that I have given to my icon is too hazy, too blurred."

"If you had waited a little longer, you might have attained your ideal."

"Yes, I did feel once as though I had got the glimpse of my ideal in a certain individual and I went drifting towards that. I went closer and closer to the figure but......but on observation I found that my icon was not there, that was only its replica. I could neither draw back nor go forward. I could not even fall down unconscious like Moses."

Mrs. Nixon was lost in deep contemplation. Her eyes were fixed on his face but she saw nothing. Her own face was calm but a storm was raging within her. After a while, she cupped his face in her hands and looked deep into his eyes. Before she could say anything, his lips made a movement– "Mary!" The flood he had held back so long broke all controls and he wept as if his heart would break.

❑

8

It was August and the peak of the rainy season. The senior Cambridge girls planned a picnic. Some teachers accompanied them and they took train from Jutog to Summer Hill station. From there they went round the Viceregal Lodge Hill and then down to Glen. The path to the Glen was risky. It was a narrow track scattered with pine needles and dry cedar leaves. It had rained a little earlier, so the path was slippery. On the left was a steep hill and on the right a fathomless abyss. The passage was broad enough only for one person to go along and it was not possible for two persons to walk side by side by holding hands. As they were going down, misty clouds gathered up out of the abyss and soon enfolded the landscape. Nothing was visible beyond two or three yards. The girls took hurried steps downwards. They almost ran so as not to keep their feet at a place long enough to slip down. Raminder was not worried about them but Jasbir and a couple of other mistresses had lagged behind. They took hesitant steps and nearly fell at times.

'Glen' was a deep ravine and a streamlet flowed through it. The tall trees around caused a slight chill in the air and created a romantic darkness. Where large stones obstructed the flow of water, it collected in the form of small pools here and there and then went down uproariously. Many tourists sat round those small lakes. Raminder was on the look out for a secluded place. They went further down but small groups of people had been sitting everywhere. An American couple was dancing to the tune emanating from a record-player. Empty bottles of Sherry and Beer lay scattered there. Some girls encircled the dancing couple and started clapping. In the meanwhile, the rhythms gained momentum.

They all sat down under a cluster of Peach and Apricot trees. The tempting aroma of coffee wafted through the air. The eyes regained their lost lustre and the tongues, glued with fatigue, were loosened. They started chirping with regained energy. Some of the girls sat down near the transistor while others drifted far into the woods, looking for wild flowers. The mistresses started taking snaps of the rocks that outlined human forms, the maize fields on the slopes and the soft silvery bloom on the snow-covered peaks.

Raminder felt out of place in that atmosphere full of gaiety. He quietly slipped away. Crossing the streamlet he went up the hill on the right. A little way up, he stopped. In front of him were the vast grounds of Annandale Race Course. Above that could be seen the Kaithu locality and then on a steep hillock perched the Grand Hotel. Crowning it all was the Jakku hill, around which the town of Shimla had come up. Oblivious of everything, Raminder was lost in the admiration of the spectacle in front of him. To the left, opposite Jakku and behind the Summer Hill the sun, a red ball of fire, was drifting down. A thin, mauve veil had spread over the distant valley. There was a heaviness in the atmosphere, drowsy with thick fumes.

Suddenly melancholy crept into his soul. He became acutely conscious of the exigencies and difficulties of life. Love for the opposite sex was not perhaps the cure but it could at least take the sting out of the aching limb. The pain did not vanish, it mitigated its intensity, though.

Shadows: A Love Story

"Recite a couplet, please." Jasbir had stealthily escaped from the group to be with him for a while. His depression deepened on her joining him there. He cast a flitting glance at her. Then he smiled and resumed his gaze at the embers of the setting sun. When she persisted for a couplet, he recited one by Firaq Gorakhpuri, in keeping with his mood:

Sham bhi thi dhuan dhuan
Husn bhi tha udas udas
Dil ko kyee kahanian
Yad si aa ke reh gyeen
"The smoky eve, the wistful beauty
The heart was filled with memories past."

Raminder was silent. The hissing of the brook became louder and the darkness went deeper. The silvery ball of the moon, hanging from the sky, was gaining lustre every moment. He heard a sob, perhaps Jasbir was crying. Crying, he thought, was not imperative but then, what was the harm in it? The sob rose again and pricked his conscience. He turned aside a little and discovered that Jasbir had left the place. He turned further back to find Amarjit leaning against a tree-trunk, crying. This surprised him a lot and he went across to her. She went on crying. Raminder took her hands and pulled her up. She got up and clung to him, crying still. The experience was unusual for him. He made her sit on the stone which he had been occupying earlier:

"What's the matter with you, Amarjit?"

"........." she did not speak.

"It's silly to go on crying like that."

"I.......... I love you, but you.....you", she blurted out but at once bit her tongue and hid her face in her hands. She was no longer crying but was absolutely still. Raminder felt sick with self-pity. He had never tried to know what went on in the heart of this young, delicate teenager. After what she had said just then, everything became clear to him and some past incidents flashed across his mind.

A few days back Amarjit had rendered a song for a cultural programme in her school. The magical note in her voice had enchanted everyone. The lilting melody was still fresh in his memory and he could almost hear it even then. As she sang *'meri manzil aap hain'* (thou art my destination), her eyes were riveted on him. He could unmistakably feel the intensity of that gaze on his face.

"It was a beautiful song", he had said at the end of the concert. In reply her eyes fluttered and her lips quivered but she said nothing.

"Your voice is as good as Lata's."

"But not as good as Jasbir's." On hearing this, Raminder's gaze had settled on Amarjit's face. Her cheeks burnt red, her lips quivered and tears welled up in her eyes. He put his hand on her shoulder and pressed it gently. That touch, perhaps, broke her already snapping restraint. She clung to him and started crying into his coat-collar. People were leaving the hall. Though they had been standing near a rose-bush, wrapped up in the protective veil of darkness and there was no risk of being noticed, yet there was every chance of someone coming that way. One could draw any conclusion, seeing them together like that. He had come to that spot because he had asked Jasbir to meet him there. He had always wished to put a red rose in her hair-bun and he wanted to do so that evening. But before Jasbir could get away, Amarjit had followed him like a shadow. He found himself in a strange fix. Amarjit was sobbing, making his shirt wet with her tears. The warmth of her breath reached the skin. He tried to push her gently back, but she tightened her clasp around him.

Raminder's heart at once surged with tenderness for her. His fingers started combing her hair. Amarjit stopped crying and, gradually, her sobs also subsided. Suddenly, she removed herself away, cast a shy glance at him and walked away slowly back to the hall. Later, when he met Jasbir, he forgot all about putting a red rose in her hair-bun.

He also remembered that once when he had taken her copy-book to check it, he had found a blue envelope in it. The letter was an expression of a beloved's longings for her lover. Next day, when he questioned her about the letter, she cast her eyes down but said nothing. When he adopted a stern attitude, she told him that a cousin of her had made her write like that. Raminder's anger gave way to a smile. He tore the letter into bits and said, "I trusted you with a better sense than others." For a few days after that she did not attend the school and later refrained from talking to him for a month. During that period she stared at him quietly and averted her gaze when it met his. Whenever he talked to Jasbir, she made it a point to pass by them. Jasbir had many times drawn his attention to her piercing glances. Raminder found her behaviour a little abnormal. It was a sign of premature awareness of the physical aspect of love. He had never realised, though, that she loved and deified him.

❑

9

Raminder had gone to Jalandhar only for a couple of days but returned after a month. He was down with fever the very night he reached Jalandhar and was confined to bed for about three weeks. Then he returned, much against the doctor's advice.

He reached the Convent when the prayer period was almost over. He went straight to Mrs. Singh's office. His colleagues came to meet him there, but Jasbir was not with them.

He learnt from Mrs. Nixon that Jasbir had got engaged and was getting married in the near future. He felt as if a great load had been taken off his chest. After ages he found himself a carefree man, with not a single worry in the world. He felt as if he had been suddenly released from an iron cage or a prison cell. He was reminded of Synge's *'Riders to the Sea'*. The old woman had lost five sons at sea and when her sixth and the last one also met the same fate, she heaved a deep sigh: 'One after the other all of my sons have gone to join their forefathers. Now I have nothing, whatsoever, to worry about. In spite of all the storms in the sea, I shall sleep in peace. What more the sea can do to me now, when there is no one that I shall have to weep for!"

That day in the Convent he had a feeling of elation. In the class he kept telling tales from Shakespeare or quoting Ghalib

Shadows: A Love Story

or narrating Vincent Van Gogh's love-affair with Kay. In the evening, he went to Shimla with Mrs. Nixon and Master Sharavat. They viewed an English movie in 'Regal', and then walked up and down The Mall for some time. They went to Cafe-De-Park and occupied cane chairs under umbrellas. Relaxing in the green round garden-chairs of the Cafe, they watched people walking up and down the Mall. Later they sipped cold coffee and took hot dogs. They laughed and smiled merrily as though they had not a care in the world. They had their dinner at the Kwality's and then walked back enjoying the moonlight. After covering the three-mile distance from Shimla to Boileauganj they went round the Karera Devi hill and reached 'Tawi'. There they took tea at a road-side restaurant and then started for Jutog through the Tu-Tu bazaar. On the way Raminder asked Sharavat about Miss Ranchan. He chirped, "Oh, now it's a matter of a few days only."

"Really? Then you deserve to be congratulated." Raminder's smile had no guile.

"Optimism is also a malady", Mrs. Nixon said testily.

"Mrs. Nixon, you don't know the real situation", Sharavat retorted.

"Why not? You never can reach that girl's heart–not in this life at least." There was anguish in her tone.

"Separated were we for ages, O Lord! Let this life of mine be dedicated to you." Raminder quoted "Vaani" in a sing-song way. None spoke after that and only the sound of their footsteps could be heard in the stillness of the night.

On reaching his room, Raminder suddenly found himself in low spirits. He felt as if he were slipping down into the depth of a well where it was all dark and damp. He kept on sitting in his chair for a while. He became suddenly conscious of losing something precious. What was it, he had no idea.

In fact, he knew what he was losing but did not want to admit it. He opened a drawer, full of letters. White, blue and pink envelopes peeped out of it. He read some of those letters and then started staring blankly on the wall opposite, unconscious of his own being, only his mind was weaving his thoughts into a web.

Earlier he was not sure that he loved Jasbir really. He considered it enough to indulge in small talk, to exchange letters and to express his views in a forthright manner. Beyond that he had never bothered. He had never tried to fathom his love for Jasbir. At times he felt that she was the right sort of a girl for him, her heart was pure and her love selfless, but her parents could never get used to their relationship. He often wondered how her mind could develop so well in such a stifling atmosphere. He wanted Jasbir to be his own but at the same time desired to have no connection with her people. It often occurred to him that Jasbir appeared so perfect and enchanting to him only because of the romance in the atmosphere, and after their marriage she would acquire imperceptibly the middle class ethos that had always antagonised him–the same hypocrisy, diffidence and narrow-mindedness. When he pondered over this, he was almost contemptuous of her. For days together he did not talk to her, didn't even reply her lettered, kept away from her–but then, one day, he would feel forced to go to her, to talk nonsense to her and to quote romantic Urdu couplets. Jasbir would complain, shed tears, regret his indifference and bemoan her own helplessness. Then, the sweetness of her smile wiped out all the traces of bitterness and they parted with promises of steadfast love, all over again.

During all those meetings, not even once had he mentioned wedlock, nor had she ever given a hint for that. They were lost in the buzz of their passion, their hearts were beating at the same rhythm and their thoughts were the beads of one

Shadows: A Love Story

string. When he learnt about Jasbir's proposed marriage he realised that he was being deprived of something that he had cherished so long–nay, for ages. Something he had always preserved in the secret chamber of his heart and in the reservoir of his emotions.

The well was getting darker and darker and he was being submerged in that darkness. The bottle of whisky lay half-empty but it was the burden of thoughts that made his eyes heavy. The failure in love squeezed his blood, drop by drop. How could it be that Jasbir was going to be someone else's? Then the realisation, that he too considered woman a thing that had to be possessed, irritated him. It was preposterous to regard the possession of her as his right. It amounted to invoking the right of possession when a house in the neighbourhood was being put up for sale. He lived in her thoughts, wasn't that enough? But that was also, in a way, an exhibition of his ego. He took pride in her love for him but was not impressed by it. A dewdrop trembled on the petal of rose but it was incapable of getting absorbed in that.

Raminder had a long pull at his whisky and was at once filled with contrition. It was a delusion and an attempt to cover up his weakness. What would have she felt like when she had agreed to marry someone else? In which drug or whisky could she have found escape from the tortures of her mind? This thought depressed him even more. He got up and went out as if in a dream. The night was dark and misty, filled with an air of frustration. He got drawn towards the Oak View Cottage. He knocked at the door. Someone turned in the bed and the dim light of the table-lamp spread in the room. The curtain was removed from the window and someone peered into the darkness, of which Raminder had become a part. He stood still, his eyes wide open but was lost, sinking into a sand-hill. The curtain came back to his place, the table-lamp was switched off and the person went back to bed. He sat down against the verandah wall. His body was burning and his eyes were heavy. There was a hammering in his head while someone was pulling at the strings of his heart.

The next evening, Jasbir came to see him. For long they remained listless, saying nothing. She kept on gazing at the calendar on the wall opposite: Finding Krishna engrossed in his flute, Radha was about to go away when Krishna held her by the arm. Jasbir was looking at Krishna's fingers, digging deep into Radha's arm:

"Did you have to decide it all so suddenly and secretly?" Raminder asked, looking at the ceiling.

"Negotiations had been going on for quite sometime but I had always rejected the proposal. When you were gone, I felt abandoned. On their persistence, I kept quiet. My silence was taken for my consent and it was all decided." Her eyes were still focused on Krishna's fingers, pressed on Radha's arm.

"You should have, at least, asked me."

"Asked you what?"

"Didn't you have confidence in my love?"

"I could not reach the depths of your love and was ashamed of the scantiness of my own. Moreover, you had said many times that marriage was not the goal of love."

"I never said that it was not. I must have said that it could be but it was not essential that it should be."

"Yes, you said it was not essential but I think it is an absolute must."

"All middle-class girls think so and you are one of them."

"I can't help being one."

"But you can rise above them, you can take a broader view of love and life and understand their relationship."

Shadows: A Love Story

"I have loved you, that's an eternal truth."

"Won't you love the man you are now going to marry?"

"I may love him the way I loved you but I have never been able to give you the kind of love that I shall give him."

"Why?"

"Because you always lived in my dreams and my thoughts but could never commune with my feelings. You became a deity and established yourself on a high pedestal and I could worship you only from a distance. I could not ascend that pedestal because I was unsure of my capability to do so. My body was only a body, after all, and not a spirit like yours."

He huddled near her. For a while, they were silent and then his fingers went into the soft flesh of her arm. Jasbir's gaze shifted from the calendar to the fingers on her arm. Then she looked at Raminder and saw a desire, a pleading and a pain in the contours of his face. At once she felt inert and utterly helpless. He kept on watching the fluttering shadows of long eyelashes on her pink cheeks. Then he bent down and touched her eyelashes with his lips. The whole atmosphere got enveloped in a grey mist. The sea-waves kept striking against a rock, the flame of the lamp flickered in the wind and then–a firework burst in the air and countless tiny stars went flying all around.

❑

10

The train was moving. Silence pervaded the compartment. The blanket had slipped off Jasbir and she was fast asleep. He realised for the first time that she had become even more attractive, after marriage. The whole compartment vibrated when the train changed tracks and a lightning sensation ran though Jasbir's limbs. He thought of the time when this body had been so close to him. Hadn't it become his own for ever, after that? What does it matter whether a body is in close propinquity to someone or not? Body is only a shadow of the soul, an obstruction in the fusion of two flames. Actually, he thought, consciousness was everything. That was the only reality; all other things were mere illusions.

That evening was still wrapped up in an amethyst twilight. The loud rhythmic note of their bodies had suppressed the sweet melody of their souls. He remembered the letter she had written after that evening–"I lay considerable emphasis on the need of the moment, for that is the essence of life and that alone is progression but it does not imply that consciousness should accept defeat and loosen its rein. In fact, separating body from consciousness amounts to picking a flower from its stem and its roots. Consciousness emanates from the body and then becomes its cradle to rock it."

"That evening you accepted me, body and all. That moment released my arrested self and from then onwards I

Shadows: A Love Story

could tread the long path of life with a clear conscience and face all the struggles involved. I am, now, free from all mental pressure and strain."

The child suddenly cried, perhaps due to the weight of the blanket. Jasbir took him in her lap. Raminder, unaware of his surroundings, was staring at the wall opposite. He had written in reply: "After the physical contact, you may be feeling liberated, your personality may have undergone an evolution, but I feel like a lone star that has broken away from the earth and is rotating in the hemisphere. My existence, in itself, is meaningless unless you condescend to make it purposeful. Now I am like a wave held in the mid-air, incapable of advancing and incapacitated to retreat."

The train came to a halt in a wilderness. The engine whistled. The child was still asleep. Jasbir looked at Raminder but he had his eyes fixed on the wall opposite. He felt on his face the prick of her glance, but he was, sort of, immune to it. He was silent but his consciousness was wide awake, it was fluttering like a bird whose wings had been clipped:

"How did you feel when you burnt all my letters?"

"How do you know?"

"It was my wedding night. You kept reading them by the fireside and then you threw them into the fire, all my letters torn into bits."

"I was not in my senses then. My world had collapsed."

"But when had you really made a world for yourself?"

"It was there in my heart, in my mind."

"Then how could such a world be ruined?"

"The mirror of the mind had no image of the outside world. It was blank."

"You wept, Raminder, after reading that letter—why?"

Shadows: A Love Story ● 51

"You had written therein that you could discard the whole world but would never leave me."

"Was there anything wrong about it?"

"You had also written that you could survive on sighs and tears provided I were with you on this journey through life."

"Didn't you believe me, then?"

"Then, yes."

"And now?"

"Now I feel it was only mawkish sentimentality."

"Wasn't it a bend in the road or a sort of milestone? Wasn't it the crystallization of a complete moment?"

"But, Jasbir it was only a shadow, like the flitting shadow of a wandering cloud."

"Yes, it was a shadow, so to say, but of some reality."

"But now?"

"Just as childhood is now only a shadow for us, youth will be the one when we get older. But these, Raminder, are the shadows of life, illusions or reality."

"What about all those pledges and promises of yours and bonds.....?"

"They are still there. The moments when we yearned for each other are standfast in their places. They are the milestones on the path of our love."

"That means we did not then comprehend our sentiments, did not examine them thoroughly. If we had, our promises to live and die for each other would not have gone up in smoke."

"Raminder, yours is a pessimistic approach–at every moment, at every hour, life is on the move. Everything around us is changing: we are changing, our views, our feelings, our objectives are undergoing a change but this change, this transformation, does not prove that all our previous feelings and aims were false and delusive."

Shadows: A Love Story

"If they were not mere delusions, how is it that we are now totally different from our earlier selves?"

"We are, now, what we were then and shall remain so in the future as well."

"What do you mean, Jasbir?"

"We are travellers on the beautiful but difficult path of life. Some incidents, some people become milestones on this path but we are not immobilised with them, we do not cling to them. We are always on the move while they are stationary, but the attachment and love that we develop for them does not wane, it can never wane."

"But what about those poor milestones......"

"They are, Raminder, the throbbings of our hearts and the essence of our existence."

"Isn't that enough for the whole of our life? Isn't it infidelity to be in search of other milestones?"

"If life is on the move and if there is progression, new milestones will come up on our paths. Their lack in our lives would be an affront to the former ones."

"But, Jasbir, certain milestones mark the end of a journey and become destinations in themselves. There are certain moments that stretch over the whole of our lives and thereafter–"fancy no more roams abroad."

"Actually, no moment and no hour is greater than life itself, even though that moment contains the full image of the life to come."

"Jasbir, I take a different view of life. A moment can hang over my life for ever, weaving a web over it in different hues and patterns till eternity."

❑

11

It was October and a heavy sadness weighed over the Jutog Cantonment. Many army officers and jawans had gone to the NEFA and Ladakh borders. A wave of anger and resentment had risen among the people against the Chinese aggression. The atmosphere in the Convent too had undergone a change. Almost all the children belonged to army families. The faces of all of them were tinged with sadness but still there was a peculiar gleam in their eyes.

Raminder had just reached the Convent, one day, when Amarjit approached him–slowly and hesitantly. Her eyes were swollen and her face withered:

"Sir, will you do me a favour?"

"What?"

"Will you come with me wherever I ask you to?"

"But where?

"Far, far away from here?"

"Amarjit, you have gone crazy."

"Sir, please come with me to the NEFA border where my Daddy has gone. I'll shoot the infernal Chinese there. Won't you come with me, Sir? Please–"

Amarjit covered her face with both hands, perhaps she did not want anyone to see her crying. She did not want to be weak at that crucial juncture:

Shadows: A Love Story

"When did your Daddy go?"

"Last night at ten and I kept weeping throughout the night."

"It is cowardly to cry at this time and it does no good to anyone."

Raminder had said so only to pacify her. Crying indeed was not proper but the next moment he thought that the suppression of tears would nevertheless be more hurtful. Crying at such a moment indicated that the delicate bonds of human relationship are threatened to be broken and one is pulled by some stronger strings to the altar of sacrifice for one's motherland. These tears are the outcome of only a moment of weakness and the next instant they become the fountainhead of the desire to give a rebuff to the enemy. This desire then becomes a passion.

In the evening, he went to Amarjit's house. Mrs. Grewal was serious alright, but not depressed. On seeing him a smile appeared on her lips, a nameless smile:

"Major Grewal didn't even meet me before leaving."

"He got his orders only last evening and he left at night." She motioned him to take a seat.

"One cannot even be mentally prepared to leave at such a short notice."

"That does not go for the army people. They are always ready, mentally as well as physically."

They were sitting in cane chairs in the lawn. It was getting dark and cold. Thin smoke arose from the tea-cups. All of them were quiet and lost in their own thoughts, but the strings of their hearts were vibrant. A glow-worm came near their table, revolved round it once or twice and left. Their eyes pursued the tiny spot of light for sometime and then it disappeared:

"I beg leave of you now." Raminder got up from his chair. Mrs. Grewal asked him to stay on for dinner but he politely declined the offer. Amarjit came with him upto the gate. There they stopped for a moment.

"Amarjit, that day at the picnic you said that I didn't love you and cared nothing for you....."

"Sir........" She could not speak, only her eyes were fixed on his face.

"Silly girl? I love you very much, very, very much!" Raminder placed his hand on her shoulder and then passed out of the gate in big strides. His attempt to hold back his tears was not very successful.

❑

12

Jasbir's wedding had to be postponed because of the Chinese aggression. She was very sad during those days. In her vacant periods, she was rather quiet and avoided meeting Mrs. Singh. Whenever she saw Mrs. Singh, she felt herself cringe. Ever since Jasbir's engagement, Mrs. Singh had become very nice to Raminder and whenever she showed him undue indulgence, he drifted mentally away from her. He had never bothered much about her jealousy and rancour for Jasbir. His sympathies were with the latter but he believed that it was a dispute between two women and he, as a man, was incapable of comprehending it.

That day a national leader was to address a gathering in Shimla. The Convent had been closed for the day and all the teachers and students had gone out. Raminder was also leaving when Mrs. Singh called him. The accounts of the money collected for the Defence Fund did not tally. He had spent an hour in checking the accounts on her table when she said–

"Raminder, you are eating your heart out for Jasbir; Isn't it?"

"No, not exactly–I am only a little depressed."

"I must say, she did not reciprocate your love."

"Mrs. Singh, I could not comprehend the intensity of her love. She kept seething within herself but could never express her state of mind."

"Burning within oneself or fluttering like a nightingale– these are outmoded terms and not in keeping with the modern times."

"The greatest tragedy of our times is that our feelings and thoughts are still in tune with the old values, but the time has changed. Our concepts of love, marriage and morality also need undergoing a transformation, accordingly."

"You should marry a smart girl."

"Marry or love?"

"Love and then marry."

"You mean a marriage, with love as its preface?"

"Yes, precisely–a type of love that should gradually lift the curtain off from the tableau of marriage."

"Jasbir's love was absolutely selfless."

"Perhaps it was not love at all. Why did she give her consent to be engaged to someone else?"

"For the simple reason that I was not sure how intensely and how deeply I loved her."

"She was sure, on her part, of her own feelings. Isn't it? Then why this somersault?"

"She knew that but her love could not go with a begging bowl to someone. She had an individuality of her own which she did not want to lose. Her love was proud of its vanity. Could she relegate her vanity to the background? If she had done that, what would have been left with her?"

"She could have had your love."

"Mrs. Singh, what does it matter whether you get love or not? Her love for me was an image of her own love. My identity was only a mirror in which she saw that image."

Shadows: A Love Story

"Raminder, I don't believe in such philosophical conjectures. I consider love only a double-edged weapon and nothing more."

"A weapon to lift the curtain off the tableau of marriage !"

"You are very naughty." She got up from her chair and came near him. In the meanwhile he too left his seat. A smile flickered on her face and she encircled him with her arm. In the batting of an eyelid, she kissed Raminder ardently and then left the room hurriedly. He flushed with anger and embarrassment like a child who had been forcibly kissed and then jeered at.

❏

13

One day Raminder got a letter from Jasbir. She had written, "Love is not a flower, and if it is so it grows on a stem full of thorns. Had that been all, it were nothing; but now I realise that love is a fire that keeps smouldering in the minds of the persons in love. I have nothing against anyone. I am what I am. This is a truth as my love is the truth in itself, and nothing on earth can make me deny it. In this, I can never be deceived or cheated."

"It is next to impossible for me to forget your love or to be devoid of its warmth. When I say that you are mine and only mine, I do not want to be content with a shadow. My existence is complemented by yours. I am like the moon that has to get its radiance from the sun of your personality. I can love you but not your memory. This is a fact. When I have to decide whether I shall lead life nearer to my heart's desire or as the people want me to, I shall find no difficulty in choosing my path, my destination."

Raminder went on reading it for long. He was confronted with the problem of a very strange nature. He did not want to be disappointed in life. He did not deny the multi-faceted charm of life but never believed failure in love to be the end of the romance of life. He loved Jasbir no doubt but only one aspect of his personality could get attached to the process of love; the rest of

Shadows: A Love Story

it was attracted by various other charms the world held for him. But when he learnt about Jasbir's engagement, all the aspects of his personality centred at one point and he frantically craved for Jasbir to be his own. If it could not be so, life for him would become a long stretch of the desert, the wilderness. He could then think of only one thing–could she be his?

Jasbir was sizzling in the fire of her own passions. She had faith in the truth of Raminder's love, but was unaware of its depth and extent. Now, with a gesture of love from him and with a peep into the mysterious chambers of his mind, her own love had flared up into a blaze. It was as if a sandalwood forest had caught fire and, surrounded by its fragrances, someone exclaims–'The flowers appear to be on fire!'

Raminder read out that letter to Mrs. Nixon. She listened quietly, with rapt attention. Then she said laconically, "Jasbir has gone crazy in her love."

"Mrs. Nixon, what if we couldn't belong to each other?"

"Love is a sacrifice, a keenness to lose oneself in someone else."

"That's sheer idealism, Mrs. Nixon. My love is on the look out for a solid base. It's desirous of finding an idol–so that I may see it, feel it and call it my own–my very own."

"Your love is only a lump of flesh that pulsates. This pulsation is very powerful. No argument, no logic can distract you from its charm, its fascination."

"My love is not mere lust, Mrs. Nixon, it has an aroma of pure passion and selfless devotion."

"Raminder, would it be possible for you, in case you do not marry her, to feel the fragrance of your beloved in flowers, trace the flicker of her memory in the twinkling stars and be conscious of her existence in the very breath of yours?"

"No, Mrs. Nixon, I can't do that, I shall never be able to do it, and I don't want to do it. I cannot make someone's memory a part of my existence. I can weave flowers in her hair but can never smell in them the crushed and stale odour of love. I cannot stand to see the ideal of my love superimposed on the satiety of someone else's lust. I am a man, Mrs. Nixon, not a god."

Back in his room he kept writing till late into the night. It was a letter to Jasbir: "I can wait for any number of years, even till eternity. Don't think what your people will say, what others will think of. Try to imagine, if we could not belong to each other, what havoc would the coming years play with our lives? Won't we find ourselves shut in a cage of our own making? Then we'll merely strike our wings against the bars of this cage and shed tears of blood. What would then become of our lacerated feelings?

"I am prepared to make any and every sacrifice. I know my responsibility and am conscious of your limitations also. I do not want to do anything in the rush of emotions. I blame no one for the present situation, for there are many forces at work. We cannot, however, rule out the possibility of an explosion that may put an end to this ritual of action and reaction—in fact, we should be prepared for it."

"I also realise that this desire in me, of making someone mine, is a sign of that primal stage in the evolution of human species when body occupied the first and the foremost position in man-woman relationship. At that stage all that man could do was to possess someone once and for all and no one else could dare to put forth any claim to it. Man jealously guarded woman—why? Not that she was weak and helpless, but because he considered her his personal property—one of his most precious possession."

Shadows: A Love Story

"I often wonder at the motive of love that I feel for you. Do I consider you my possession or my property? It will be no exaggeration if I say that you are my very life, the throbbings of my heart. All this sounds very poetic, indeed. But then, poetry is the true image of reality. At times it transcends reality. But I wonder wherein lies the truth. I only know that I love you and that your love complements mine own with its presence. I am not alone in this struggle–you are with me. Without the assurance of your love, I am nothing and my love has no base to exist on."

"Love is not a bond, it is a discipline; it is not an overflow of feelings but a principle; not a legacy but a challenge. If one can attain love and maintain one's individuality also, it is a victory, a great victory. Living as the shadow of someone else's personality is mere detachment from one's self. Love involves attachment but not detachment from one's ownself."

❑

14

Raminder was taking his class one day, after the battle of Bom De La, when he noticed Amarjit. She was crying. The book was lying open before her on the desk, her eyes fixed upon it, but tears were streaming down her cheeks as though she had no control over them.

After the period, Raminder called her to the staff room. By then, tears had dried up on her cheeks but her eyes......!

"What's the matter, Amarjit?"

"We got a letter about Daddy yesterday.........."

"What..........what has happened to him?"

"He has been missing for some days."

"Missing? Where's the letter?"

"At home. Ever since Mummy has been crying inconsolably."

"Take courage–You can go home, if you want. I shall come over in the evening."

Amarjit's eyes were wet once again. He left the room. If he had remained there a little longer, he wouldn't have kept himself in check. He did not want to shed tears–not for a brave soldier like Major Grewal. Moreover, he had only been reported missing.

In the evening, he went over to their house. Some people were already there in the drawing room. He occupied a chair

Shadows: A Love Story

outside in the lawns. Dry leaves were scattered everywhere, some of them had got stuck up in small flowerpots. It was autumn and the whole place was enshrouded in a melancholy atmosphere. The air had the chill of sighs and the dampness of tears. He turned aside a little and noticed Amarjit sitting on the ground near him. She was absolutely silent. Her face was expressionless and her eyes held no question in them. When Raminder placed his hand on her shoulder, she leaned against him and her head rested on his knee. He kept watching the flowers and dry leaves in silence. The sun had set and it was getting dark. The buzz of conversation ceased in the drawing room. Slowly and quietly, someone came to stand by him. She had a smile on her face–a smile that muffled all the sorrows and all the despairs of human existence.

"Why are you sitting outside, Master Raminder?" Mrs. Grewal asked him.

"Solitude enables one to think clearly. One can at such moments peep into one's heart", he replied while getting up from his chair.

Amarjit drifted towards her mother and then they all went inside. It was slightly dark in the room. Amarjit switched on the light and drew the curtains on the windows. The room became cosy. Mrs. Grewal and Amarjit occupied the sofa and Raminder took his seat opposite to them. He had a good look at Mrs. Grewal and felt himself small. On her face was only a mist of worry and brooding but no lines of sorrow:

"Amarjit told me there was to be a farewell party in the school this evening."

"Yes, Jasbir's farewell party is in progress right now."

"Aren't you supposed to be there, too?" You have a sort of right to do so."

"What right? To attend the farewell party or something else?"

"Take it anyway you like, but you should have gone there."

"In fact, bidding farewell pains me a lot."

He wished he had not said that. Tears came into Mrs. Grewal's eyes and her gaze was intent on Major Grewal's photograph on the shelf. Amarjit had in the meanwhile fixed her glance on Raminder's face, as if she were listening to him not with her ears but with her eyes. Her face expressed her sadness and her whole being was shrunk and wrapped up. When Jasbir's name was mentioned she felt as if someone were pulling at the strings of her heart so strongly that they had nearly snapped. Some airy fingers had produced vibration in them and reawakened in them a melody that had long been mute.

"Miss Jasbir is getting married in a few days." Amarjit said as if to herself. Raminder looked at her but kept quiet. Mrs. Grewal appeared to have heard or seen nothing. After a few minutes she got up and went to the other room. Raminder saw her leave the room and he realized instantly that those who struggle in life also know how to accept the inevitable. He was deeply impressed by this aspect of her balanced personality:

"Sir, why didn't you marry Jasbir?" Amarjit's eyes betrayed wonderment.

"Was that very essential?" Raminder said that for the sake of saying otherwise he knew the hollowness of his assertion.

"Didn't you love her?" She persisted in her eagerness to know the reality.

"It is not necessary to marry the person you love." His voice was feeble for want of conviction.

Shadows: A Love Story

"Now, after Miss Jasbir's marriage, would you be able to love her as before and consider her your own." Amarjit's body had assumed the pose of a question mark.

"I will go on loving her for ever." He was finding it difficult to stay there any longer. He knew the state of her mind and feelings. He was also aware of the frustration Amarjit had experienced in her half-blossomed love, when everything was enveloped in a thin layer of romantic mist.

"But, when you will meet her after her marriage, I mean a long time afterwards, would you refuse to recognise her? Would you break all links with her and behave as if you were complete strangers?" Amarjit was digging her nail into a painful spot in Raminder's vein. Perhaps she wanted to know whether the pain was due to her probing or the vein itself was throbbing with pain.

"I consider love a process to attain equilibrium in one's personality." Raminder was standing on a dune which was drifting every moment underneath his feet. As he tried to take his feet out, he went deeper into it.

"Sir, tell me, is Miss Jasbir your ideal or the image of your ideal?" Her eyelids flashed rapidly. "Amarjit !" He blurted out in a sad tone but then kept silent.

He got up and proceeded towards the door. Going down the veranda-steps, he looked back and saw her silhouetted in the door, perhaps an image of his own conscience.

Later, as Raminder opened the door of his room, he stumbled against an envelope. He pressed the switch but there was no light. After much difficulty, he found a torch. He placed it on the table and its light fell on the ceiling in the form of a circle.

He felt tired and extremely weak. He lay down on his bed and opened the envelope. It was a letter from Jasbir : "It's 2 O'clock in the morning and I cannot have a wink of sleep. Life has become a burden for me but I am constrained to live.

You were my first love and will remain my last too. Now, after this, I can never love anyone else. Fragrance will no more emanate from the close touch of someone else. Nor will there be the ringing of a thousand tiny bells in my ears at the approaching footsteps of someone. I shall spend no sleepless nights for someone nor shall I wait for anyone to visit the land of my dreams. Now there will be only my ownself and the boundless desert of my life–stretching out to eternity.

"I have no interest in life now. Someone is going to marry me but I shall not be able to give him happiness. The colours of the rainbow of my life have run riot. They can never be sorted out nor can they be set in their original order. They can never be reconstituted for me in a swing to dream in and to find my dreams realized. Something has snapped within me– its echo will always resound in my ears but no one else will ever come to know about its existence. Someone, not a human being but an unseen presence, has stabbed my soul and it will henceforth keep writhing in pain. It will groan but never complain–never expect sympathy from anyone.

"I have learnt that you will not be there at my farewell party. Will you not fix into my hairbun the red rose that was rooted in our love and thrived on our hopes?"

Raminder sat stolid for long, after reading that letter. He kept thinking of his life, his love and his future. His hopes, his aspirations lay dead before him. He took out of the drawer all the letters that Jasbir had written during the last few days. He picked one out of them–"What can happen at the most? I am not concerned about my life, but it is impossible and meaningless for me to go on living without you. I inhale your name with every breath and will go on doing so for ever. My own existence does not matter. I am only your shadow. I am always with you in light as well as in darkness. I am a part of you, an inseparable part."

Shadows: A Love Story

"I had not craved for flowers when I ventured on the path of love; I had only dreamt of them. Now, when I find my path strewn with thorns, I am not disheartened. You had a talk with my Daddy that day and I realized that he was a part of the traditional concepts and could not be weaned off from them. If only he could put himself in our place, our problems would have been solved and our desires fulfilled. That day, and afterwards too, I tried to impress upon him the need for a change in his outlook. Mummy too did her best but to no avail. Perhaps, the generation gap makes all the difference. He does not want me to be yours because you admire Mrs. Nixon and consider her chaste while she is living with Master Sharavat. He wants his daughter to have nothing to do with the people from a different stratum of society—exotic and outlandish.

I have decided that I shall never be disloyal to you even if I were to die a spinster. I shall be nobody else's but yours. For you, no, not for you but for the culmination of my own love, I shall face every hardship. I shall live for you and for our bond of love—love that is eternal."

Raminder read another letter and then another—one by one, he went through them all till it was early drawn. His eyes started closing with the fatigue and weight of his sorrow. A line from Urdu poetry flashed through his mind: *'Tera khyal jaage ga, soya karenge hum.'* (Your memory will keep vigil, while I am asleep.) It kept revolving in his mind like a big dragonfly that enters a sick-room on a hot afternoon and keeps flying about till the eyes of the patient begin to close by themselves.

❑

15

The train was running very fast, as if in a desperate attempt to get rid of its destination and to go to a place where there were no regrets for not having reached the destination. Why should one bother about destination when it is sufficient to tread, with blistered feet, the path strewn with thorns? The lovers had been transported to dreamland. Not reality but fantasy had occupied their minds. They drew closer to each other in imagination, in a sort of fantasy while their bodies were undulating on separate berths:

"Jasbir, are you happy, really happy?" said Raminder, touching her soft round arm with his burning palm.

"Yes, very happy." Jasbir placed her hand on his but neither of them spoke for a long time. Their thoughts were reeling back at that time but they were also aware of the time leaping forward every moment. They were lying face to face, though at a distance. Raminder's hand was digging into her arm and the back of his hand absorbed the warmth from hers.

"But you told me you could not live a moment without me, could never belong to anyone else." He felt irritated at his own question. It showed that he did not share her happiness. Perhaps, in his heart of hearts, he still wanted her to pine for him.

"Do you mean I should light a lamp on the grave of my love lost and sit beside it to keep its flame alight with the oil of

Shadows: A Love Story

my tears? No, I could never do that. My love is alive and it will never die." Her body trembled like the flame of a lamp on a stormy night.

"Then, your love for your husband is merely mundane, with no touch of your spirit in it?" He was conscious of the futility of such a puerile curiosity.

"I cannot see the body and the soul as two separate entities. When I suffer some physical pain, my soul also winces and when my soul is hurt, my body knows no respite, either." Jasbir sat up and looked, not at him, but out of the window. Outside, sparks flew out of the furnace of the engine and were getting lost in the air.

"O yes, now I recollect, you once said that our love was like a milestone on the endless path of life." Raminder's gaze rested on her face for a while and was then dissolved in the mistiness of the years gone by.

"If our love was once, headstrong and impetuous like a mountain stream, it has now gained the steadiness of plains. But it is the same love, its source is the same, though it has changed its pace." Jasbir tried to round off the discussion. Neither of them spoke for sometime. Then Raminder asked:

"How did you discover that?"

"I had discovered that in the veracity of my love."

She put her head on her raised knees and then encircled them with her arms. The edges of Raminder's eyes were wet but he did not want to wipe them off. He was looking at Jasbir, at that beautiful mellow body undulating in the gentle currents of her sobs.

❑

16

Raminder drew aside the window blinds. Outside, a sheet of snow had covered everything. The sky was still overcast with white clouds and it seemed that snow would start falling again. It was the first snowfall of the season.

He made himself a cup of coffee and settled again in his bed to drink it. He found its aroma very pleasing and wished he could go on drinking the aroma itself instead of the coffee. Then it struck him that one could not survive on aroma alone and for that matter how long could fragrance last? Such ideas irritated him. He often thought why he could no longer live in the world of romance, as in the past. Why he had to come back to reality with a jolt. Why could not this real world turn romantic or the romantic become real?

He put his cup down and picked up a book lying nearby. He was turning the leaves as yet when someone knocked at the glass-pane with a finger:

"You are still asleep?"

"The day hasn't dawned yet."

"Oh yes ! After all, the day doesn't dawn as early as nine O'clock in the morning?"

"A whole lot of snow on your coat ! Is the snow falling again?"

"No, I was coming down a slope when a branch overhead waved all its snow onto me."

Shadows: A Love Story

"Oh ! Have some coffee?"

"No, let's go out for a walk."

"In this cold weather."

"It is not cold at all. Come out of the bed and see for yourself."

Raminder took a deep sip and put the cup down on the saucer. He was about to pick it up again when Jasbir took it up. She had a sip out of it and then put it back on the saucer, held in his hand. Their gazes met. The balls of Jasbir's eyes danced with joy and a smile lit up her face. Raminder smiled back at her and felt as if someone had touched a string inside him. For long he could feel its vibration and hear the melodious notes it produced. Then he felt as if his love had not yet nurtured. It was full of passion alright, but it lacked mental poise. Love may be exuberant and wild like a boar, but at times it needs be guided by the dictates of the mind.

It was so calm and still outside. Their feet were sinking into the soft, white snow. Sometimes the foot went so deep into it that it became difficult to take another step. On crossing the Jutog bazzar, they took the path that led to the 'Arki' village. The snow was not so deep henceforth. Going down the steep footpath they just about managed to avoid falling down but they were unconcerned about their safety. They felt like two explorers set out in search of a new world and a new age. After a while, it started snowing and the snowflakes got stuck to their clothes. Deep silence prevailed all around. When they talked, their voices seemed to be coming from a distance and those were not easily recognisable.

Snowfall became heavy, they stopped under a tree. The village 'Arki' was discernible in the valley ahead and its housetops were under the thick layer of snow. The clouds had lowered further. Tiny flicks of snow danced, before their eyes, to the beat of some divine rhythm. Raminder looked at Jasbir. Her eyes gleamed and there was a rosetint in her cheeks but her smile betrayed the troubled state of her mind. They both stood there for a long time–aloof and far away from the madding crowd.

Raminder's heart vibrated with the fervour of his love for Jasbir. He wanted her to turn into a statue so that he could worship her for ever. He wondered why the Greek sculptor had to invoke God to infuse life into his statue. If he had loved his creation intensely, he would have created a great many replicas of the same. Instead, he wanted life to be infused into his creation. His wish was fulfilled but the woman he created perished after sometime. On the contrary, Raminder wanted Jasbir to turn into a statue and become the deathless object of his love.

Jasbir's lips were absolutely cold and he wondered if she had already been turned into a statue of ice, beautiful but remote. That Greek statue would not have pulsated with life at such a short interval as his beloved had assumed the form of a statue. But the statue was lifeless. He touched its lips. They were cold but the breath was warm and soothing. He clasped the statue hard, too hard and the snow started melting under his palms:

"Time to make a move," Raminder suggested looking at the snow-covered pine branches above.

"Yes, it has stopped snowing." She removed her gloves and put them in her pocket.

"Need we go to Arki now?"

"You wanted me to see the pond there that freezes during snowfall and turns into a good skating rink."

"But now it's the time to go back. If it starts snowing again, the path would become hazardous."

Going up the slope was not so difficult. They walked together holding each other's hand. He thought it would be wonderful if she could hold his hand and walk with him like that for ever. Before going back to the Jutog bazaar they turned to the track leading to the European graveyard. Jasbir had no intention of going there. Why spoil the pleasure of hiking in such a pleasant weather by visiting as dreary a place as that? But Raminder was, somehow, keen on going there. They started walking single, for the path ahead was narrow. Raminder had purposely chosen this one instead of the broader one. Jasbir was finding it hard to keep her balance. She was scared, so she sat down. Raminder went ahead, not knowing that she was not following him.

There was a big heap of snow in front of the graveyard gate. He did not go in but perched on the boundary wall. At that time he noticed that he had left Jasbir far behind. He signalled her to come up. She got up, went back a little and took the broader path down. She was taking cautious steps and her arms waved in the air as she tried to keep her balance. She put one foot forward into the snow and then carefully lifted up the other one. Raminder intently watched her coming down. The feeling he had then in his mind was by no means that of tenderness:

"You are a typical middle-class girl," he told her when she joined him.

"How?" There was a crack in her voice.

"You can only tread the ready-made, beaten path."

"Why find new ones while you have set paths before you?" Her face flushed with anger while her eyes were misty.

"Many people in the world have over the years loved each other. Then what's the need for the freshers to love?" He said more to himself than to her.

He was sitting near Jasbir but was mentally far removed from her. He was unaware of her presence. He had gone down into a marshy abyss, where there were no wild roses but only dry leaves, no cool breezes but mere humidity. He held her hand in his–it was lifeless. He enclosed her in his arms–it was only a body, one among many. This thought made him shrink back just as a tortoise withdraws itself into its shell at an unknown touch.

He kept on wandering for a while among the graves, which had been buried under many layers of snow. Roses and Dahlias, growing nearby, were feebly peeping out of the snow. The projecting branches of the trees were covered with snow. When a branch stirred, a whole heap of snow fell down, causing a mild snowstorm, so to say.

He spread his overcoat under a tree and lay down on it; melancholy weighed heavy on his heart. He felt like a lone wanderer on a deserted island. He remained lying there for sometime, with his eyes closed. Then he looked towards the place where Jasbir had been sitting. She was not there. He again closed his eyes. Suddenly he became restless and got up with a jerk. When he advanced towards the boundary wall, he saw her climbing up the slope, step-by-step.

❑

Shadows: A Love Story

17

"Mrs. Nixon, has Master Sharavat gone somewhere?" Raminder enquired, entering the room.

"Yes, he has gone to Miss Ranchan. She has invited him to tea," Mrs. Nixon replied while putting on her gown.

"So, his yearnings are on the verge of being fulfilled." He sat down on the sofa and switched on the radio. Mrs. Nixon smiled in reply.

As he took a magazine from the rack and started flipping through its pages, Mrs. Nixon took up a novel. A Western tune from the radio filled the air in the room. He glanced at Mrs. Nixon who was engrossed in her book. He took off his shoes and stretched himself on the sofa:

"Feeling sleepy?"

"No, sleep is gone with her!" he sighed.

"Have you any regrets?"

"No, none whatsoever."

"Then, why can't you sleep?

"Because I keep on thinking about her."

"Why this obsession?

"No, Mrs. Nixon, it's not the case. I am worried about her. She may commit suicide."

"She is not such a coward," Mrs. Nixon raised her voice and added, "Miss Ranchan, who attended her wedding in

Ludhiana, told me that she was fully composed at the time of her marriage."

"Yes, Mrs. Nixon, she must have been but I just cannot stop thinking about her."

"You are much too sentimental," Mrs. Nixon told him. Raminder did not say anything but closed his eyes. He felt very weak and tired. For long, he remained still. Mrs. Nixon went back to her book—perhaps another love-story, more interesting and more fascinating.

"Raminder has just gone to sleep, don't wake him," Mrs. Nixon told Master Sharavat as he entered the room.

"He is awake already," Master Sharavat chuckled as he said this.

"Have you met Miss Ranchan?" A smile played on Raminder's lips.

"Mrs. Nixon, you tell him everything about me." Master Sharavat protested.

"I asked her myself. Why be so secretive about it?" Raminder raised himself up.

"I tell you, Raminder," finding Mrs. Nixon concentrating on her book, Master Sharavat whispered, "she has gone all nuts over me now."

"How?" Raminder asked.

"She complained to me that visiting her place on her invitation was no visit; I should meet her of my own accord."

"So, that's it ! What else did she say?"

"I have dated her for the movie; you are welcome to join us."

"Why should I join you?"

"Alright, we'll join you, then." Raminder smiled wryly in reply.

❑

18

Raminder told Mrs. Grewal that the names of the Indian personnel in the custody of the Chinese were to be broadcast that night at quarter past nine.

"I know, Master Raminder." Her face was as blank as a sheet of paper.

"Sir, Daddy's name is going to be there."

"Let's hope so!"

"You are perhaps going to Dehradoon tomorrow?" Mrs. Grewal asked him.

"Yes, tomorrow, by the night train."

"Are you joining the Public School there?"

"Yes." During the ensuing silence, Mrs. Grewal went to the kitchen. Amarjit brought out her carrom board. She beat him at it several times. She was happy to win and he was happy in her happiness:

"You are losing on purpose."

"Does anyone ever lose on purpose?"

"Why not? They are the greatest winners who lose purposely."

In reply, Raminder looked intently at her. She had averted her eyes but everything was clear on her face. Raminder stood up. He wanted to go, but then he remembered that he had to listen to the broadcast at quarter past nine and it was only half past eight as yet. Mrs. Grewal invited him to dinner and he could not decline the offer. He remembered the day he had come there on Amarjit's birthday. It was all so cheerful then. He had the glimpse of a new world in the company of army officers and their wives. He had discovered a new vista of life.

At nine, they sat around the radio. News was being broadcast in English. The Govt. of India had received some lists from China. They were not giving full information about the Indian prisoners but were sending small lists at short intervals. Names began to be read out at quarter past nine, about fifty or sixty of them, but Major Grewal's name was not there.

The radio was switched off. Silence weighed heavy in the room. All three of them were lost in their own thoughts. They did not see one another. Silence was interrupted only by the clicking of the clock on the shelf. Its red secondhand pushed time ahead, slowly but certainly.

The calendar fell down from the wall and the window again banged close by itself. He looked at Mrs. Grewal. She had sunk into a corner of the sofa and her eyes were closed. Amarjit was crying, her sobs rising into the air. Raminder left the room. There was a dense darkness outside. He had come into the dark from the light, so his eyes were dazzled. He stopped a while in the verandah and turned to find Amarjit standing there. He started going down the verandah steps and she too walked along with him. He stopped near the gate:

"Sir, are you leaving now?"

"Yes."

"When will you come back?"

"Can't say. Perhaps never !!"

"No, sir, I shall never let you go, never !!"

"Don't be silly." Raminder patted her cheek. She was trembling like a dewdrop on a leaf. Suddenly, she put her arms around him. She lifted up her inquisitive eyes. Raminder, in momentary dizziness, took her in his arms.

She was trembling and kept on trembling against his chest for long. His lips were testing the salt of her tears and he could see lotuses afloat in the pools of her eyes. Then her trembling ceased and she withdrew herself from his clasp. She walked back like someone held in a dream:

"Good night, Amarjit."

"Good night, Daddy."

Raminder remained rooted to the spot for a while. Her words echoed in his ears, "Good night, Daddy–Good night, Daddy." Then he heard a door slam. Before long the shadow, clinging to his feet, stretched itself out and started moving with his steps.

❏

19

The train had slowed down. Everyone in the compartment, except Raminder, was asleep. Jasbir had covered her child fully with the blanket and was herself without any cover over her. The soft sound of her husband's snoring was audible. A milky bulb shed dim light in the compartment. Outside, a row of lights came in view. The train halted at a station. Raminder lifted up the shutter and peeped out. He was alarmed when he read the name of the station. He dressed himself up quickly and collected his bedding and suitcase. On opening the door of the compartment, he quietly slipped his holdall down on the platform. Picking up his suitcase, he alighted from the train and rushed to the waiting room. He placed his things there and returned. He stopped in front of the compartment which he had lately left. He peeped through the glass-pane. Jasbir was fast asleep. He saw the shadows of her long eyelashes falling on her cheeks–the fine needles of her eyelashes fell apart, even in their shadows.

❑

Shadows: A Love Story

Lingering Pain

(a novella)

One

As Rama turned her side in bed, her hand rested on her husband's shoulder. She pondered over for some time whether to withdraw her hand or let it remain there. In fact, there was hardly any difference between the two situations. He was in deep sleep. Rama had been aware of Randhir's nature for the last three or four years. They went to bed at night at about eleven. As soon as he lay in bed the savage in him woke up and his body became unbearable for Rama. After the stormy condition, he turned his back on her and went into deep sleep. She considered herself at that time like a wild animal, whose male came out of a bush, pounced at her and after satisfying its lust, moved away to some other side. Rama was lost in a vacuum thereafter, and her mind turned into a deep mire in jungle. Her thoughts got entangled. She had been unhappy at Randhir's sex hunger of this nature; her soul remained dissatisfied and her emotions, virginal.

She was in a very strange condition that night. Her brain was like a station through which an electric train passed making a hissing sound and soon after the passing of the earlier train, another train came in hissing. Pinpricks were tormenting her, her temples were burning hot and every pour of her body was scorching her. She pushed aside the quilt, switched on the table lamp and took a draught of water out of the golden glass

Shadows: A Love Story

pitcher lying on the table. Her heart was pounding. She got up, opened the door slowly and went out.

There was moonlight in the lawn. Cool breeze was lifting the veils off jasmine buds. There was a sort of intoxication in the atmosphere, as if a spell had been cast over it. She stepped out barefoot and walked on the grass covered with dew, her soles absorbed the coolness of the earth. Gradually, she regained her equipoise, her feelings threaded into a chain. Her eyes got drenched in tears which flowed down her cheeks and then fell on the grass— perhaps the dew was getting its debt repaid.

❑

Two

It was the beginning of November. Air had become cool. The leaves of apricots, peaches and apples were turning pale. Some leaves flew into the air with a little gust of wind and then slowly fell on the ground. There was not much of a hustle and bustle in Shimla those days but this lack of hubbub had its own charm. The song of autumn was more enchanting than the melody of spring. The fragrance of the wild roses blended in the morning air, the weather got more pleasant at mid-day and the warmth of sunrays subdued the coolness for some time, but the evening air became biting. Soon the entire atmosphere was enveloped in the grey sheet and the snow on the peaks of the surrounding hills started shining brightly.

Such were the days when Rama came to Shimla for the first time. She had been married a few days earlier. Randhir was working as an engineer in Shimla. His leave had not yet expired — he still had ten days or so. How romantic were those days! They were feeling carefree. Everything seemed beautiful. They got up late in the morning, gossiped for some time, and the process of kissing and hugging continued. Sometimes they took an hour or so to leave the bed. Then they had bed tea. They left their place at about eleven, when the sunshine was bright, but the surroundings appeared to be dozing off and half-sleepy. The dry leaves rustled under their feet as they walked. Rama enjoyed walking on dry leaves,

Shadows: A Love Story

and had a feeling of some rare joy. After some time, they moved about on the Ridge. Their eyes remained fixed for long spells on the horizon at the snow-capped peaks. When a gust of wind disheveled Rama's hair or a lock of hair came down on her forehead or the corner of her sari slid down her breasts, they exchanged glances and smiled. Walking arm in arm, they moved towards the Scandal Point. Very few people were generally standing there at that time. Because of the winter days, most of the tourists had gone back. Women came out for shopping at that time and stopped at the Scandal Point for a while. They talked of one thing or the other and many new scandals came into existence.

They stopped there for some time, looked at the people going along the Mall and then they moved towards the Telegraph Office. The road from the Telegraph Office up to the Grand Hotel was their favourite stretch for strolling. Walking along, they remained absorbed in talking. A little hint or a small indication caused a furore within them and if the road was empty at that time, Randhir pinched Rama's flank or encircled her waist with his arm or clasped her. Rama shied a little but never much. Firstly, the road was almost empty at that time and secondly, they had no idea that someone was looking at them. They thought why should anyone take interest in them. Everyone seemed to be busy in their own way. Lost in each other, they reached gradually the Chaura Maidan. Generally they returned from there and went to the Coffee House. They liked to drink coffee at that time or sometimes they had hot dogs or hamburgers. They spent half an hour or so there and looked at people sitting at other tables but soon they realized that those people had fixed their eyes on them. Thereafter, instead of looking this way or that, they looked at each other. When Rama smiled, a dimple appeared in her left cheek. For Randhir, there was quite a lot in that dimple. He deliberately talked of something which brought a smile on Rama's face and the dimple got deeper....

They had their lunch at Kwality Restaurant. They liked food at that place. They returned from there after three. They got seated in the chairs kept in the lawn of their lodge. They glanced through the Filmfare, the Eve's Weekly or the Readers Digest or related to each other something that had taken place before their marriage. They laughed over everything and smiled over nothing. After some time, they felt the keenness of the sunrays and, placing the magazines on the chairs, they went into the drawing room.

Lost in each other, they lay down on the sofa for quite some time. Then the evening, collecting all the colours in the corner of its scarf, reached there. Randhir got dressed up in his fine suit, Rama wrapped herself in a sari. Generally she donned a half-coat or a Cashmere shawl. They went to the Mall for evening walk. There was a good crowd there at that time. Men and women walked arm in arm. Some couples seemed to be quite unmindful of their surroundings. They got lost in the crowd. They realized then that life was multifaceted and a special feeling attuned them with one another. They felt the chords of their hearts touched by a common current.

They had dinner at nine, after which they had Espresso Coffee and then walked back to their lodge. In the heart-warming atmosphere of the night, Rama's boat seemed to rock, as if caught in a tide, and then it reached the bank with the push of a strong current. Rama wished that those days should never come to an end; should remain so for ever, unchanged — but it was her wishful thinking.

❑

Three

Randhir had resumed duty. He had his breakfast at nine and left for office. His lunch was carried to office by the servant. They had their evening tea together at five thirty. For Rama, those days of waiting were very tiresome. Her imagination followed Randhir the whole day. She smiled when she recalled what he had said or done to her, feeling shy and shrinking within herself. She started ambling in the lawn at five. The footpath which linked their lodge to the road was visible from there. It was a five-minute ascent. Rama had a special attachment with the footpath. On both its sides were the apricot, peach and apple trees and one or two plum trees were also there. Their leaves were falling off those days. Going up or down the footpath, Rama entwined her arm in Randhir's, but he wriggled out of her hold slowly and encircled her waist with his arm. All her weight leaning on his arm, their steps got unsteady.

Sometimes, returning from the evening walk, Randhir lifted her up in his arms and ascended the footpath. One of Rama's arms was round his neck. He felt tipsy at that time. When she waited for him in the evening, her eyes remained fixed at the footpath. Recalling such moments, her cheeks reddened and a smile appeared on her shy lips. At that time, instead of looking at the footpath, she turned her eyes towards the slope to the right side of the house. The slope got lost in the trees on the edge of a deep ravine. There was a steep ascent again and the hill beyond was snowpeaked. The sky seemed very close from there. Sometimes she felt like reaching the snowpeak and touching the sky.

As Rama was lost in such thoughts, there was some rustling on the dry leaves. She looked back and saw Randhir coming up the path. Both of them smiled and the next moment Randhir's lips were pressed on Rama's.

Sometimes Rama was out of sorts suddenly, though there appeared to be no rhyme or reason for her sadness. Sitting alone or looking into the distant space or reading some book or a magazine, she used to feel dejected, as if a stray cloud had come over the shining sun. Something seemed to scrape her heart with sharp nails or clasped her brain tightly. A steam emanated from her heart and a sigh escaped her lips.

She was extremely happy before her marriage. The colours of the rainbow had filled her imagination. Her friends shared jokes with her, teased her again and again. She felt at ease with their jocular taunts but furrowed her forehead to pretend her unconcern. Randhir had seen her for the first time when he had come to Delhi. Her mom and dad went to the railways station to receive him.

At that time her younger brother, two years younger than her, said– 'Take Didi also with you....' Rama had frowned at him but his eyes were full of fun. Her mom and dad smiled. She returned to her room pleased with herself. How joyous was their household that day! Rama was trying to engage herself in one thing or the other as if to escape from herself. Time had become a big drag. The ticking of the clock was unmindful of the palpitation of Rama's heart. Hearing the arrival of the taxi, she went to the balcony....A young and healthy man of medium height was with her mom and dad. She stepped

Shadows: A Love Story

back. After half an hour, Rama, her younger brother, her dad, her mom and the guest occupied the drawing room to take tea. Rama looked towards Randhir once or twice and then lowered her eyes shyly. Randhir talked to her a little– the subjects she had in her B.A., her hobby, her interest in music, etc. Rama enjoyed giving replies to such questions. Most of all, she liked Randhir's way of talking– he had an equipoise and was blessed with suave manners. This was their meeting before the marriage.

They were married. Rama remained caught in the whirlpool of her emotions for three or four months and she received all the comforts of life from Randhir. But she had started feeling depressed without any reason. She was aware of some kind of emptiness in her life. She could not give a name to this sort of emptiness. She had a word about this with Randhir also. He reassured her that one might feel a little out of sorts in those days and after the childbirth, her state of mind would again get normal. Rama was expecting a baby. She was nurturing a little life within herself those days. She was not convinced of what Randhir had told her but she kept quiet. She gave birth to a baby girl in September. For Randhir, it was a very happy day. Rama too was no less happy. The child was the living sign of their love.

❑

Four

Rama had begun to feel rather seriously that her physical and mental satisfaction had taken wings. Whenever she accompanied her husband for a dinner, she came across some people whose only aim in life was to seek pleasure. They were always on the look out for some little opportunities to have physical satisfaction. Rather they created such opportunities themselves. She felt pained on realising that for those people, she was not Rama but one of the beautiful and enchanting women in their circle.

She came in contact with the wives of high-ranking officers and leading businessmen and their daughters in the Snow Club. She was greatly surprised to start with when she came to know that Mrs. Khosla and Miss Khosla were entangled with the same man and both of them were successful in their own way. Once a very delicate situation had arisen. At a function of the Snow Club, Mr. Khosla, Mrs. Khosla, Miss Khosla and that man were present. After the evening tea, variety programme started. A one-act play was to be staged. Mrs. Khosla and Miss Khosla, both of them were taking part in the play. Mrs. Khosla had to come to the stage twice in different dresses. After the first role, when she went into the green room to change her make up, the young man also went in with her. Meanwhile Miss Khosla did her small role and returned to the green room and saw the youngman standing behind the

Shadows: A Love Story

curtain with his back to her. She clasped him from behind and dug her teeth into his back. In the confusion, Mrs. Khosla and Miss Khosla collided with each other and the youngman, who had gone nonplussed, advanced towards the outer door hurriedly, while Mr. Khosla was entering the door at that time.

Rama chanced to meet another young girl, Miss Rakshi, in the club. She was a very clever and sharp girl. Rama had come to know that about two years earlier she had been swinging in the arms of a married man and when he divorced his wife, she also broke with him and got involved with another married man. When Rama met Rakshi, she was enticing a third married man and raising her swing of love high to reach him. On seeing Rakshi's spotless face and innocent lips, Rama felt like ignoring all the scandals to get closer to her — but she could not drive out of her mind the idea that Randhir too was a married man.

Another one was Mrs. Ghabghab. When she came in their midst, there were smiles all around. She had a buxom body, enchanting complex, tall and blooming. Mrs. Ghabghab was as much popular among women, as among men— rather more. Her husband was a government contractor and he generally remained out of station. Mrs. Ghabghab had been rarely seen with him. It was learnt that he had married his sister-in-law at the age of 40, after the death of his wife, when the sister-in-law was only eighteen years old. When Mrs. Ghabghab came to the Snow Club, she shook hands with other ladies or said 'hello', but she hugged Rama affectionately. For Rama, such a show of affection was rather obscene. As soon as she saw Mrs. Ghabghab, she wanted to hide somewhere— but beautiful objects could not escape her attention. Rama was in her embrace the next moment and her forehead or cheeks were stamped with her burning lips.

In the annual function of the Snow Club, all the ladies were at liberty to bring along their partners. Rama reached there with Randhir. The young ladies had their partners with them. Balloon Dance was to be performed before dinner. Fifteen to twenty couples came to the dance floor. The ladies were holding very large balloons and men's arms were around the waists of their women partners. During the dance, when the tune was changed for a moment, many hands were extended in an effort to pinch the balloons. While the men were trying to pinch the balloons of other couples, they were also mindful about saving the balloons of their partners. When dance returned to the previous tune, the couples who did not have the balloon, quit the dance floor. Ball Room dance continued for five minutes or so and then the tune changed suddenly — the balloons got burst and the dance was resumed. At the end, there was only one couple with their balloon in hand. That couple was presented a large trophy.

Rama, who had declined to join the balloon dance, was watching the entire spectacle sitting with Randhir. She was not unaware of the fact that all the men were trying that their hands might reach the other balloons or not but must be rubbed against the protruding frontal assets of the women. On the other hand, the women, in trying to save their balloons, acted in such a coquettish manner or made such eerie sounds that the dance turned wild. After witnessing all this, Rama stopped going to the Snow Club. Randhir wanted Rama to get acquainted with the style and manners of high society, but she stuck to her stand. Her mind was not ready to accept all that sham show of genteel society and she finally decided to bid goodbye to the club.

❑

Five

The loneliness of Rama's heart continued to increase with each passing day. Her restlessness in Randhir's presence escalated all the more. As long as he remained in the house, he hovered around Rama's body — he kissed her, or took her in his tight embrace. Sometimes she woke up with a start. Her mind and heart revolted against his behaviour. After he left for office, she felt that she too had an individuality of her own; her tall and lissome body really belonged to her. She could sit or lie down anywhere. Her longings became intense on such occasions. She wanted someone to talk to her, to ask her to sing a song, and move along with her on desolate paths. She had a keen desire to sit in the lawn during moonlit nights. The moonlight, sieving through the pine trees, fascinated her. John Keats's poem *'Ode to a Nightingale'* was very dear to her heart. She contemplated a nightingale singing soulfully at a distance, and the atmosphere surcharged with intoxication. Some fingers may comb her hair and her head may rest slowly on someone's chest, the time should stop its pace, those moments may become immortal, and the emotions may reach their peak. Sometimes she felt like going out on a fresh morning and climb the top of a hill and watch the scene of the first sunrays spreading over the hills. She had a very keen desire that some day the early sunrays should kiss her eyes, and tickle her body. The redness of the setting sun in winter lit countless lamps in the corridors of her mind, and every hair on her body trembled. The last rays of the sun bloomed pink flowers in the snow on hill peaks. The white line, touching the horizon, turned crimson.

She felt sad all the more during the snowfall days. The feather like flakes of snow fell down slowly on roof tops, electric wires and leafless trees and dressed them in white apparel. She liked very much the snow settling down on trees. When the wind whistled in the fireplace, she wanted that someone should come and sit with her on the sofa, talk to her softly, and relate to her the tales of the distant past and the unknown lands. Both of them should continue to gaze at the smouldering coals in the fireplace. Their lips may be sealed but their minds need be in conversation with each other. When the hissing of the wind increased the stillness of the night, she may hold the hand of the dear one. Her heart should pound loudly and her head lean to rest on his chest.

Countless thoughts of this type swirled in her mind. Initially she asked Randhir to look at the spectacle of sunrise but, for him, getting up before eight, was not only difficult but impossible.

'This is Shimla, not Delhi. If you go out early in the morning in this cold weather, you will have pneumonia.......' was his patent reply?

During snowfall, Randhir occupied his seat close to the fireplace, sipped whisky, read American novels and teased Rama. If Rama started her talk about something romantic, he looked at her disdainfully as if she had committed a crime. She had unwillingly stopped talking in that manner.

Randhir was very happy that his wife was beautiful, they had rented a tastefully decorated lodge 'Craig Du' and he had a good job. They had engaged a maid to look after the

Shadows: A Love Story

baby. The cook was already taking care of the kitchen. Randhir's health had improved greatly. He had an impressive personality. He had changed his routine after the child-birth. Instead of coming home directly from office, he went to the club, played rummy or bridge, took whisky, burnt cigarettes and sometimes got an opportunity to sit close to 'someone'. He valued such occasions and for a colourful evening, he could blow up a lot of currency notes. He was very happy that his wife knew nothing about his secret life. He returned from the club at ten or eleven at night, and after taking his meals, lay down in bed. His sleep was disturbed in the morning only when the servant knocked at the door to bring in the tray of tea. Winking his eyes, he looked at Rama lying beside him. Then he placed his burning lips on hers. Rama got up with a start and rubbed her lips with her hanky for quite some time — as if a lizard had clung to them.

❏

Six

One evening, as Rama had gone for a walk on the Mall, she met one of her old friends. Both of them were together in college and they were closely attached to each another. Shashi was with her husband— a young man of slender build. His eyes exuded wisdom. She came to know from Shashi that Naresh was a professor who taught English in a college in Shimla and they had been married for about two months. Rama congratulated her. Shasi introduced Rama to Naresh with these words:

'She is Mrs. Rama who has done B.A Honours in English literature. She had won many prizes in the literary competitions held in the college. Besides, she is fond of singing and….' perhaps she would have said something more when Rama interrupted her–

'Where is the need for such an introduction? Tell me something about him also. ….'.

Looking at Naresh, Shashi added,

'He is a lecturer in English literature. He passed his M.A. two years ago– First Class First. Now he is doing Ph. D. Two collections of his poems have been published, etc. etc.' Shashi had a hearty laugh after saying this. Naresh and Rama also joined the laughter. They walked together on the Mall for some time and enjoyed the renewal of their friendship.

Shadows: A Love Story

It was the month of May. The hustle and bustle at the Mall was at its peak. The way from the Scandal Point up to Kwality Restaurant was like a river that had two waves which passed side by side in opposite direction— one facing the North and the other, South. The Northern wave turned into the Southern wave on reaching the Scandal Point and the Southern wave turned into the Northern wave near the Kwality Restaurant. This started at the evening and continued till late in the night. People did shopping also inbetween or entered the Coffee House or had tea at a restaurant. They then joined one or the other wave, which turned into the second one after some distance. Rama had so many rounds of the Mall after a long time. In a very short time, Rama and Naresh got thick. They talked about many things, starting with English literature and ending with the suggestion for Mutton Dosa. Rama had agreed to go to the Coffee House at the instance of Naresh:

"Three Mutton Dosas and three coffees"

Naresh gave the order and in the white tube light he observed Rama's face on which melancholy had cast its net.

❑

Seven

'We are late by one minute and fifty seven seconds. Don't mind much…..' said Naresh entering the drawing room of 'Craig Du.'

'But according to my watch, you have come early by three quarters of a minute,' replied Rama with a smile. The smile had the bloom of the jasmine buds, opening their petals. When she had met Shashi and Naresh three days ago, it had never occurred to her that there would be a welcome change once again in her life. She had invited Naresh and Shashi to tea in the evening so that she could introduce them to her husband. Randhir did not go to the club on Sundays. He came into the room a little after they had arrived. They said 'Good evening' to one another, shook hands and after saying 'How do you do,' they sat down. They talked about Shimla weather and also the impending snowfall. The good quality of tea was praised and Randhir went away after that. He had to attend a party at a friend's place and it was very important to go there, according to him. After he had gone, Rama, Shashi and Ramseh came out of the drawing room and occupied the balcony:

'Shashi, that yonder hill peak starts having snowfall from October itself and when the sun sets in the evening, its crimson light, falling on the snow, presents on enchanting spectacle,' said Rama pointing to the hill to the right of the lodge.

'This peak must be shining in the moonlit night also,' said Naresh taking recourse to his imagination.

'At that time I feel like going there to be on the top of the hill, and have a look at the world to my fill, walk on the snow till late in the night, and keep bathing in the showers of the moonlight and my crystalline feet should never tire of walking there.'

Rama had got lost in her thoughts. Naresh thought, 'How much yearning is there in her words and how much disappointment in her tone and tenor!' Some unknown power brought Naresh very close to Rama. He felt as if he knew Rama for ages, was aware of the touch of her breath and the dimple in her left cheek…he did not want to think beyond that. He put a heavy lock on his thinking. And taking the notebook out of his pocket he said–

'I will just read out a poem.'

As he read the first line, Shashi said, 'Not like this. Recite the poem in your sing-song voice.'

'Not at this time, let it be some other time. …it is okay like this for now…'

Naresh looked into Shashi's eyes in such a manner that she kept quiet. He recited the poem. His tone was full of pathos. The pathos ignited a spark in Rama's heart. She felt suffocated and her throat dried up:

'You should also recite something, Rama,' said Shashi to her. But Rama was not in the mood at that time. But when Ramesh insisted, she agreed to do so. Rama sang Ram Kumar Verma's song–

'Chumban see chhoti hai jeevan ki yeh raat.'

(This night of my life is as short as a kiss.)

They could not see one another properly in the growing darkness. Their eyesight had gone far away into the space, trying to locate something. Their hearts were swinging to the same beat. Rama was singing in a low tone. It seemed to her that she was not singing but listening to the song– only her lips were moving. The song ended but the effect thereof remained. The words of the song kept echoing in the space of their minds for quite sometime.

❑

Eight

Rama went to Shashi's house after some days. Naresh had not yet returned from college. They kept on talking of one thing or the other. They were happy that time had brought them close to each other once again. In the course of talks, Shashi asked Rama,

'Why do you look so sad, Didi?'

'O, No. '

'Don't hide anything from me. You were not like this during the college days.'

'Leave those days alone.'

'And now….?'

'Now, you see…' Rama had not yet completed the sentence, when Naresh came in:

'Oh, so you are here.'

'Shashi told me that you come back home at three.'

'I have been delayed a bit today. There was a poetic symposium in the college.'

'Why didn't you take Shashi along with you?'

'In fact, it was a very small function. Three or four poets have come here from outside. They were invited to tea by the college and the poems were recited inbetween.'

After a short while, Rama asked,

'How do you compose poems?'

'Just…like this…nothing particular.'

'Even then…'

'When the feelings become powerful, they assume the form of a poem.'

'But why do the poets generally express in the poems their unfulfilled desires?'

'What is not attained in life, is transformed into symbols and metaphors.'

'The poets, writers and artists convert their feelings into art, but where should the other people go for fulfilment?'

In the meanwhile, Shashi brought in tea. Rama had a sip of hot tea and placed the cup on the table. Naresh was still trying to find answer to her question.

'Tea is getting cold…' Shashi reminded Naresh.

'Oh, yes.' Naresh was still lost in thoughts.

'It seems to me that this life is just an illusion…'said Rama getting down deeply into what she had said.

'How come?'

'Sometimes you think that the reality of life lies in a particular thing but after attaining it, why does one start feeling that it is just a useless thing, an optical illusion., nothing else…..'

'It would mean that life is like a diamond which is visible to all but the colours it exudes do not seem alike to everyone …some are able to see one colour and some others a different one. But everyone thinks that the colour which the other one is seeing is better. There are, however, some who can see all the colours at the same time.'

After saying this Naresh was again lost in thoughts.

'It would then mean that,' Rama's eyes were fixed at Naresh's face, 'one should not draw any meaning of

Shadows: A Love Story

life throughout one's life as nothing is true though everything is a reality.'

'This is the point of view of those who cannot understand themselves. When we think in our own way, live in our own way, the reality gets crystalised…. In fact that is the reality, all else is just deception and misapprehension.'

Rama was satisfied with this answer, but not fully satisfied. Avoiding further arguments, she stood up–

'I should better leave now….'

'Where is the hurry?' asked Shashi.

'It's getting late and I have to do some shopping also.'

'All right, we'll give you company upto a short distance,' said Naresh.

Going up the ascent, they reached the road, above the U.S. Club, which ultimately passed by Ritz Cinema and led to the Mall. On both the sides of the road, stood large pine trees. There was complete silence on the road at that time as no one was seen coming or going. They walked along silently for some time. Because of the trees on both sides, there was a little bit of darkness, but it was not yet the time for the lamps to be lit. Crickets had started making noise loudly. A tingling sensation passed through Rama's body. She realized that instead of considering life a big piece, it would be proper to regard it as consisting of small pieces. One keeps threading into a chain the small pieces scattered here and there and then one's world is complete. It is not necessary that one should ever remain in search of a big piece to make one's life meaningful. The big piece is found not only with difficulty, but it is not always a necessity. That evening spent with Shashi and Naresh was for her a small but valuable piece of existence.

❏

Nine

Shashi and Naresh visited Rama frequently. She too went to them. They had got quite mixed up with one another. When the three of them got together, it became a happy meeting for them. Naresh recited his poems, Rama sang a song and Shashi played a tune on the Sitar. This was followed by tit-bits and laughter till their flanks ached. Sometimes they played some indoor game or went out for a stroll. The long paths ended but not their talks. Naresh brought some books, a novel, or a play or a poetry book, from his college library for Rama. She read the books intently and when they met next, they discussed it critically. Rama's questions baffled Naresh. He often thought that mere study was one thing but natural talent, quite another thing. When a literary debate started between Rama and Naresh, Shashi slipped away. If she was at her own place, she went into the kitchen. When they were at Rama's place, she went out to the lawn with Rama's little daughter. For her, literary discussion was a mere waste of time.

One day they drew up a programme to have a picnic at Crignaino Rest House. Rama asked Randhir to accompany them but he excused himself on some pretext. He was not in favour of traversing such a long distance for the picnic. Ever since Rama had come in contact with Shashi and Naresh, she had started feeling better. The emptiness within her was slowly yielding place to fullness. Her cheeks were becoming ruddy

Shadows: A Love Story

and when she smiled, the dimple in her left cheek seemed deeper......Naresh had written many poems as a eulogy to that dimple. When he recited those poems to Rama, she became wistful and nostalgic. This melancholy was different from the one she had experienced before meeting Naresh. The earlier one was like the withering of a flower before blooming and this one was like an autumn evening– when the heart aspires for unknown delights.

❏

Ten

They left for Crignaino Rest House at seven in the morning. They had sent the servant and the cook by bus in advance. The baby had been left under the care of the maid. Rama, Shashi and Naresh got cycles from Lakkar Bazaar. They had planned to go up to Mashobra by cycles, and then on to Naino on foot. They could not ride their cycles from Lakkar Bazar upto Snowdon Hospital because of the steep ascent. Balancing themselves on their cycles, they started going uphill at Snowdon. Rama looked quite charming that day. She seemed to have made a special selection of her dress for the occasion. She wore a tight dress, shirt and *salwar*, which revealed the contours of her body in an ample measure. Naresh deliberately lagged behind at the ascent so as to appreciate her undulating figure. She had a slender waist and fleshy hips.... He was in for a bit of excitement. So he was panting for breath at the ascent while Rama and Shashi were going ahead of him with aplomb. They had to stop after cycling for a furlong because there was another ascent ahead of them. They walked abreast, all three of them. Shashi's face had turned red and the drops of perspiration appeared on her forehead:

'Would we have to walk up to Mashobra like this? Cycling and walking?' asked Shashi stopping under a tree.

'Oh, no–' said Rama reassuring her.

'We will ride our cycles from the next *'hawa ghar'* and there would be no need to get down again as the way ahead is just smooth.'

They stopped at the *'hawa ghar'* for about five minutes and then started cycling. The way ahead was really smooth. They were enjoying cycling. It was the first week of September; the air was still moist. It had rained the previous night and it was very pleasant indeed. The leaves had been washed and their verdure had the cooling effect on the eyes. Rama felt so nice with the cool breeze touching her face that she increased the speed of her cycle. When she began to pant for breath, she opened her lips a little and felt as if she were drinking coconut water at pre-dawn. Her hair had been disheveled and a few strands came down on her face. She had removed her *chunni* from her shoulders and tied it around her waist. All this was making the protrusion of her torso and the contours of her hips more prominent. She was cycling ahead of Shashi and Naresh, quite unmindful of them. She was aware that both of them were a little behind her. She was not ready to think of anything else. Her spirit was being carded like cotton wool at that time — light like a flower petal, pure and clean…..

She passed through the Sanjauli Bazar in the same manner. The passers- by looked back to see her, as if lotuses in their hearts had blossomed on observing her enchanting moves. They looked at one another meaningfully and resumed their journey on observing her. Rama entered the tunnel where electric lights had been switched on. As she went inside the tunnel, she shouted– 'hey….hey… hey….' like children. Her voice echoed for a while. In return she heard another sound– 'ho…..ho…..ho….' The voice was that of Naresh. Assuming that Shashi and Naresh were slightly behind her, she quickened the speed of her cycle. The tunnel ended. And a serpentine road lay ahead. On one side of the road was the rocky hill and a deep gorge on the other side. Rama had passed through this road earlier also, but she had never enjoyed so much, as she was doing then. Cars and jeeps were passing to and fro on the road. There was the danger of a collision at any bend due to a little carelessness. Rama was quite unconcerned. She was riding her cycle close to the hill, but when she had to make a turning, the cycle covered half the road in its circle. She was negotiating such a turning near Dhalli when a taxi came suddenly from the opposite direction. Rama turned her cycle towards the hill. The taxi was not running at a high speed. There was the danger of collision but it was averted luckily. She tried to control her cycle but in vain, even though the cycle was at a slow speed. The front wheel of her cycle collided against the milestone on which had been written 'Dhalli'. She fell down. Shashi and Naresh reached there immediately. Naresh helped her to get up. Her elbow had been bruised, but she had not been hurt seriously. She was smiling instead. They all walked down and reached Dhalli bazaar. They had their tea at a wayside restaurant and moved ahead.

Moshabra was not far off from there. They started cycling easily. It was a mud road. Sunshine had no reflection on the road and it appeared as if the day had not dawned as yet. Both the sides of the road were lush green. The mountain was so steep at some points that it was difficult to look up at the top. They kept on cycling at a slow speed.

On reaching Mashobra, they returned the cycle to the Mashobra Branch of the Lakkar Bazaar shop. Then they went to Mashobra Post Office and bought three inland letters. They intended writing to one another from Crignaino. Shashi should write to Rama giving in the letter her impressions of the picnic; Rama should write to Naresh in the same manner and Naresh to Rama. They wanted to post those letters at Crignaino itself without showing those to anyone so that when they would receive the letters the next day, they would know one another's mind. This was the invention of Rama's mind. Everybody liked this, as it was quite a novel idea. Rama wanted to immortalize the impression of the picnic. They bought some apples before leaving Mashobra. Passing by the church, Naresh hurled an apple into God's house:

'Why this?' asked Rama.

'For the church Padre...' said Naresh and smiled.

'But no Padre lives in this church....your apple....'

Rama had not yet completed her sentence, when Shashi interrupted her:

'Just see there...'

They spotted a monkey at a tree. It was feasting on the apple. Rama and Shashi began to clap like children and looked at Naresh gleefully. Rama took another apple out of the paper bag and handed it to Naresh with the words– 'This is only for you....forget the Darwian theory for the time being.' There was a peal of laughter.

They kept on moving and reached the Rest House before noon. There were very big lawns with flower-beds around them. Rama took many rounds of the place. Like a butterfly, she went from one flower to the other. Meanwhile, Naresh and Shashi went into the drawing room. It was a tastefully decorated hall. There were some books in a shelf on one side. Naresh read the names of books and leafed through some of them. Shashi went to the kitchen to give instructions to the cook and, on return, brought with her some sandwiches in a plate. She gave one sandwich to Naresh. He had a bite and put the rest in Shashi's mouth and pinched her cheek. When she rubbed her cheek, he said, 'You pretend to be hurt.' Then he moved towards her and placed his lips on the red mark of her cheek.

Rama was mumbling something as she walked inside. They separated on seeing her. She cast a glance at them as she entered the room and smiled. Shashi extended the plate towards her and Rama picked up a piece. Then they kept on debating whether tea should be taken in the drawing room or outside in the lawn. Rama was in favour of sitting outside in the lawn but Shashi liked to sit in the drawing room. Naresh did not want to say anything either way. He counted the merits and demerits of both the places and left the decision to them. It was decided ultimately that tea should be taken in the room and lunch outside in the lawn. Tea was brought in a little later. Shashi had her tea sitting on the carpet. Naresh and Rama sat on the sofa. Rama prepared tea and handed over the cup to Naresh who passed it on to Shashi. He took the second cup from Rama, saying, 'Thank you.' Rama smiled and the dimple in her left cheek…..Naresh realised that he was sitting very close to Rama. His right knee many a time touched Rama's left knee. They flinched for a few moments but in such way that the other one should not know. After a little while, again Naresh's right knee got joined to Rama's left…they smiled without looking at each other. Rama's cheeks were glowing. Her armpits got wet with perspiration and the cloth clung to her body at certain points. Naresh extended his arm to pick up the pastry and his nose felt the odour of her perspiration in which was mixed the fragrance of Eue-de-cologn and the reaction of both of them was quite testing for his emotions.

After taking tea, he went out and got seated on a bench which was surrounded by flower vines. He glanced at a withered rose lying on the bench. He smelled it…sharp smell of coconut hair oil entered his nostrils. He placed back the flower and rubbing his nose, he got up. He roamed about for some time and then sat down against a tree. While sitting there, he wrote a sonnet. He read it once or twice, tore it off and

Shadows: A Love Story

threw it away. Then he took the inland letter cover out of his pocket and started writing.

After writing the letter, he hesitated a bit before writing Rama's address but then he wrote the address, "Rama, Craig Du, Shimla.' After posting the letter he went to the drawing room. There was no one in the room. He lay down on the sofa with his shoes on and shut his eyes.

Rama and Shashi were walking down a narrow footpath, going down into the gorge. On both sides of the path were tall pine trees. It was a very narrow path strewn with pine straws, walking over which was a little slippery. Shashi was afraid of going ahead and wanted to turn back but Rama was keenly desirous of going ahead. Rama was walking ahead of Shashi. She sighted a plain patch covered with green grass a little away. She took a few steps ahead and then stopped. Shashi also reached her and looked over her shoulder. A boy and a girl stood at the level patch. The boy was kissing again and again her neck and the lower part of her left shoulder.

Without exchanging a word, Rama and Shashi returned from there. A turmoil was caused in Rama's mind. She narrowly escaped stumbling here and there. On reaching the drawing room, Rama sat down on a tripod near the window and looked out throw the windowpanes. There was bright sunshine outside at that time. Milk white little clouds were hovering over the hilly slopes. Birds were flying in the air. She tried to take interest in those things deliberately as she wanted to get rid of her thoughts. She could hear Shashi and Naresh talking but she was unable to follow anything. Their voices were striking against her ear drums but then those got lost in the air. The same spectacle was coming again and again before her eyes. She was feeling like a virgin who had seen for the first time a man and a woman kissing and hugging each other. Her temples were burning with the heat of her blood, her throat was getting dry and her lips were partly opened, as if she were finding it difficult to breathe through the nose.

Lunch was served in the lawn at about two o'clock. They took their meals sitting on a small carpet. They talked about a little bit but mostly their minds were preoccupied. After the meals, Naresh lay down there. Rama and Shashi also kept sitting there, with their backs against the low wall. Naresh was gazing at the yonder mountain which was without a tree and the rock had been cut in such a way as if two human forms were sculpted. Naresh drew their attention towards this spectacle. He said, 'It seems a lass was asking a passer-by to help her in placing the pitcher on her head but he was looking at her face paying no heed to what she was saying.'

'To me it appears that,' Shashi was saying, 'a cowherd is asking a maiden to dance and she, out of shyness, was looking at her feet — what do you think, Rama?'

'In my opinion a woman, seeing a man, is trying to know whether he was her ideal….' Rama stopped abruptly.

Naresh looked at Rama. Their eyes met and started probing their minds. Rama asked Naresh to recite a poem. He told her that he would recite, not his own poem, but John Keats's which reads like this:

Her soft arms were entwining me and on
Her voice I hung like fruit among green leaves
Her lips were all my own —
Ah! Ripe sheaves of happiness.

They discussed for some time those poetic lines. Meanwhile Shashi had gone to sleep and her low snoring had broken the chain of their conversation. They suddenly realized that both of them were sitting alone. Crignaino Guest House was on the back side and in front of them was a vast open space spread up to the horizon. Small rocks had risen here and there in the

Shadows: A Love Story

open space. They had been talking about one of those rocks a little while ago. Wind was hissing through the tall pine trees which were shaking from the roots to the tops. Rama was surprised how those trees had got so much of flexibility that a little gust of wind made them swing from top to bottom and perhaps centuries had passed since they had been facing the storms. They could hear Shashi's low snoring every now and then. Rama's eyes had lost their way far away near the horizon and she waited for quite some time for their return. Naresh was trying to recall one of Keats's lines.

'Rama….' The line rose up in Naresh's mind but Rama was lost in her thoughts at that time. She was startled hearing her name and looked at Naresh. Then they heard some footsteps. They looked back. A boy and a girl were walking up the footpath. The boy had one hand in his pantaloon and the other around the girl. The girl was walking, lifting up her sari a little with her hand. Rama saw that lipstick had been wiped off her lips and pine straws were stuck in her disheveled hair. Both of them passed by them and proceeded towards the guest house. Naresh looked at Rama after they had gone but her eyes were still following them–

'Yes, that line of Keats–' Naresh had not yet forgotten the line–

"Saw two fair creatures, couched side by side
In deepest grass."

'Your poetics is still going on?' said Shashi, rubbing her eyes with her palms and both of them were startled.

It was about four-thirty. They could catch the four forty-five bus. They wanted to return by bus. Rama called the servant and asked him to collect everything. Shasi and Naresh went into the room and Rama continued for some time to gather the spectacular sights in her eyes. She went in on being called by Shashi and dressed her hair standing before the bathroom mirror. The main road was at a distance of half a furlong from that place. They were getting late. Therefore, they told the servant to go ahead and stop the bus for them. They feared that if they missed the bus, they would have to traverse the long way ahead on foot. There was no other bus after that. They started getting down the slope from Naino. This was a very wide path with tall pine trees everywhere. The sky was getting overcast. The environment was getting heavy with moisture. While going down, their mood turned romantic. Rama began to sing a film song–

'The passers-by on the journey of life

Meet only to be separated again.'

Shashi also joined her. It became a gala time. They had got lost in the tuneful surroundings and when Naresh encircled one arm round Shashi's waist and the other around Rama's, nobody minded it….they had the feeling that they had left their bodies far behind.

❑

Eleven

Rama slept till very late the next day. When her sleep was broken, Randhir was ready to go to office. She got up, put on her gown and came near him. He was combing his hair in front of the mirror. Rama plucked a small flower from the flower vase, lying on the mantlepiece, and tucked it on the collar of his coat. He looked at her and smiled. He was surprised at Rama's expression of love. She seemed to be more healthy to him. Her body had become plump and supple and the corner of her lips were getting deeper. Randhir was getting late for office. He took Rama in his arms quickly and kissed her cheek. He was about to move away, when Rama held his arm and he stopped. She moved ahead raised her heels and offered her pouted lips to Randhir. The warmth and sweetness brought back the memory of the past in Randhir's heart. He held her hair with one hand and pulled those back a little and, placing his other hand on her waist, he bent down on her. Rama felt slightly suffocated.

After Randhir had gone, Rama continued to move about in the rooms. She sat down in the balcony for some time and then went out in the lawn. Passing by the dahlia-bed, she was reminded of the flower-beds at Crignaino. All the scenes of picnic passed before her eyes one by one. Then she recalled that she had forgotten to post the inland letter she had written in the drawing room of the Guest House. Then she thought that it was hardly any use posting it now. She would hand it over to Naresh when she met him.

She received Naresh's letter at 3 p.m. He had written:

'Rama dear,

Today's picnic will remain fresh in my mind throughout my life. Such moments rarely come in one's life. We had met about four or five months back and it could not be imagined at that time that one day we would get so close to each other. Sometimes I think of our mental make-up which is so similar and how our hearts beat equally tunefully! It seems that our bodies have been made of the same clay. In spite of all these things, there are some limitations between us, some social inhibitions, and our own ideals. I have been married to Shashi and you, to Randhir. I can't overlook the right that Shashi has on me. Whatever Randhir has been to you, its reality you cannot deny. I am sure such things would have passed through your mind also. But sometimes it so happens that one, knowing everything and understanding everything, cannot exercise control over one's mind and heart. I have felt many a time that we can ignore our existence to some extent but can't turn our back on it. Our existence and our bodies are stark realities in their own way.

I had applied to Delhi University some months back for a scholarship to do Ph.D. I received their approval last week. I have not properly talked to Shashi about this as yet. A struggle has been going on in my mind.... Sometimes I think of staying in Shimla but the other thought impels me to leave it. I know your mind and your emotions quite well. You want to immortalize every moment. You can maintain a distance between yourself and your ideal, can restrain yourself from crossing the limits, but I have not yet reached the peak of such self-restraint.

Shadows: A Love Story

Now when I am writing this letter, there is no upheaval in my mind. I have made up my mind to go to Delhi. I may not be able to come to meet you. I get into a strange state of mind at the time of separation. Shashi would certainly come to meet you before leaving.

Yours,
Naresh.

After reading the letter, Rama reclined her head to the back of the chair and shut her eyes. Two tears remained stuck up between her eye-lids for long and then, slipping down, fell into her lap. She had no power of thinking at that time. She could hear her heart pounding but she was disregarding its agitation. She got up and went into the bedroom. Her sobs vibrated in the air for quite sometime.

❏

Twelve

Shashi came to meet her twice after this — once at the time of Nishi's birthday and again to say goodbye. Those were all too brief meetings. A mention of Naresh was necessary but Rama did not deliberately ask her anything about him. Shashi said that he being too much involved in college affairs could not come and he had sought forgiveness.

Naresh and Shashi left on 27th September. Rama wanted to go to the railway station to see them off but the last words of Naresh's letter checked her from doing so. She did not want to put Naresh into an emotional tangle.

September had gone, and October too ended thereafter. The month of November brought back to her countless memories of three years ago. Her mind was again perturbed and her health became indifferent. There was a melancholic touch in her personality. This sudden change was like an enigma for Randhir. He kept asking Rama as to why she remained silent all the time but she had no reply to that. Randhir asked her many times to go to cinema or theatre but she avoided all that always. When Randhir teased her, instead of stopping him she started crying. She felt like crying at her helplessness. She had stopped giving a reply to Randhir about anything he asked her– she just responded in monosyllables.

❏

Thirteen

December had started. The sky was generally overcast. Life was becoming a burden for Rama. She was always lost in her thoughts but this condition led her nowhere, rather she felt unnerved all the more. She made another attempt to divert her mind and started going to the Ice Skating Rink. Sometimes she went there in the evening also but she preferred going in the morning because there was not much of a crowd at that hour. Holding a wheel chair she walked on ice. After some days, she started walking on ice without the help of the chair. She walked arm in arm with another lady friend of hers. The skates under her shoes glided on the floor of frozen ice and she moved ahead. Her left foot slipped a little on ice and then she bent her knee. In the meanwhile, the other foot slipped likewise to enable her to move forward. This continued and she had the rounds of the rink. Her feet moved on the ice and her body swirled like a gust of wind. As long as she remained there, she felt at peace with herself.

A carnival was to be held on the Christmas Day. Rama had been eagerly waiting for the day. She talked to her friends quite a lot about the carnival. It had become difficult for her to decide as to which fancy dress she should adorn on the occasion. The Christmas Day passed without the carnival. It got cloudy that day in the morning and when it was cloudy, the snow did not freeze. Therefore, the carnival was deferred to 28th December but snowfall had begun on that day also. On the artificially frozen ice, a heap of soft snow had gathered. Rama felt very bad because the event had been deferred again and again. No date was fixed ultimately. Mostly it was expected that the carnival would be held on the New Year Eve. Snowfall started again on the 31st December. It was speculated that the weather would not change for a week. Rama remained at home the whole day. She read a book sitting near the fireplace. Her feet had got so cold that sometimes she was inclined to putting them on the smouldering coals. A storm was raging outside. It was snowing heavily. The flakes of snow were gathering at the doors and windowpanes. Rama turned aside the window curtain once or twice to peep outside but she could see nothing — the windowpanes had been covered with snow.

Next day when she woke up, she discerned light filtering through the windowpanes. A current of joy passed through her body. She got up and opened the window. Heaps of snow were lying outside and the shy sunrays were frolicking thereon. A smile spread over her lips. The sky was quite clear. She phoned up the Rink Secretary. She was told that if the weather remained fine the whole day, the carnival would be held in the evening.

When she reached the Rink in the evening, her friends came to congratulate her. She looked gorgeous as Mira Bai. She had wrapped around her a yellow sari of *khadi.* She had a rosary of large beads round her neck and had held the Sitar in one hand, the chords of which she touched sometimes. One of her friends was dressed like a milkmaid and another one was attired like a Kashmiri girl. Two girls were moving around arm in arm in similar Rajasthani dresses. They were wearing long skirts and had tucked the ends of their *dupattas* into the neck of their *cholis* (blouses). A boy had become a Pathan and another one was wearing tattered clothes. He held a begging bowl in one hand, and a staff in the other. He limped as he moved. Another man was wearing a cotton wool dress from head to foot. He had a large size shoes in his feet on which wool had been glued. Two small kids were following him wearing the same type of cotton wool dress. He was a snowman with two children.

The entire Shimla city appeared to have gathered at the Rink. As they could not get tickets, many of them stood on the roadside, enjoying the scene. It seemed to be the land of Rink Fairies. Prizes began to be announced over the loud speaker. Rama won the first prize. A good many cameras clicked her. The bulbs flashed and vanished. The second prize was awarded to the lame beggar. And the third to the snowman.

Thereafter, a hockey match was played between the ladies and gents teams. The men lost the game deliberately but women felt that they had really defeated the men. The reality of life had manifested itself there also in one form or the other. Then the ballroom dancing started. The records were playing and the couples were dancing on the ice floor. Eight or ten couples were dancing in such a vast rink, like distant islands in the sea. After the ballroom dance, all the lights were switched off. Ten or fifteen torch bearing men entered the rink in a row. The same number of women came from the other side. Rama was one of them. She had tightly tied the loose end of her sari around her waist. The row of women passed close to the men and moved to the other side and began to swirl in a circle. The men too formed a circle on the other side. The two circles swirled in the rink for sometime. It seemed as if only the torches were swirling. Then the ladies' circle got enlarged. Every man moving around the circle positioned himself behind a woman. They moved in the larger circle for some time. Then they went out of the rink in a long row and the electric lights were switched on.

Before the conclusion of the conclusion of the carnival, once again they came into the rink, without the torches, and did skating for some time. Rama stumbled into a little pit and fell down. She sprained her wrist. She did not feel much in her excitement but her pain increased on reaching home.

Treatment for many days did not relieve her of pain. Secondly, too much cold in Shimla aggravated her condition. On the advice of her doctor, she left Shimla for Delhi to stay with her parents. She remained in Delhi for about two months. The time was spent in a routine manner; morning, noon and evening, one after the other.

❏

Fourteen

It was the last week of March. White, violet and pink buds had appeared on the apple and apricot trees. After some days the buds started falling down and small shoots took their place. The air contained all freshness and the warmth of the sun was increasing. Snow was still there on the Sanjauli Road but the rest of the place was clear. After the three-month long death-like lethargy in Shimla, life was renewing itself. The two-way flow of people on the Mall had not yet started, but the hustle and bustle was increasing with each passing day. The shops, which had been closed during winter, were opening one by one. The cinema houses, which had been showing old pictures during winter, had announced new films to be screened. Davicos Restaurant had opened. Its windowpanes were being given a shine. Orchestra had not yet started. Below the Davicos, Grand Clearance Board had been displayed at Janaki Das & Sons's showroom. A new mat had been spread on the steps of the stairs leading to the hall of Davicos. On the dance floor in Davicos, cane chairs of different colours had been placed on one side, and dining tables on the other side. In the opposite corner was the stage for orchestra.

Rama had returned from Delhi. One evening, she went to Davicos with Randhir. Some tables had been occupied by people. Two Anglo-Indian girls were sitting with an African man at a table. The girls were great beauties. They were wearing skirts, high-heeled sandals and red ribbons had been tied on their foreheads. They were taking Tuti fruity ice-cream and smoking cigarettes. One of the girls stood up and slowly walked to the Ladies Room. Rama viewed her gait scornfully. Another table had been occupied by a Sikh couple. The girl's dress indicated that she was a newly-wed. She was wearing red ivory bangles and her suit was of peacock colour. The girl was making a mention of 'Bhaboji' again and again, when she talked. Some people were drinking whisky on one side. They called the waiter after short intervals and gave him the orders. A blond was sitting among them. Her arms were bare up to her shoulders. She was wearing a low-cut blouse.

Randhir wanted to drink whisky but at the suggestion of Rama, both of them ordered cider. Though they were sitting close to each other, there was a gap between them which was not visible to anybody. Sipping cider, they talked of this and that when Rajan, an old friend of Randhir, turned up. He was a Captain in the army and had been recently transferred from Bangalore to Western Command, Shimla. Both the friends met each other warmly and enquired about each other. Rajan was looking at Rama again and again. 'What a taut body does she have!' This idea was swirling in his mind. The desire to enjoy that body started pulsating in a dark cell of his mind. He had established connections with some young and middle-aged bodies in the South but now he realised as if someone had challenged his manliness.

Randhir and Rajan continued drinking whisky for quite long. They would have taken more, but Rama expressed her desire to leave. They moved towards the stairs. Randhir went to the gentlemen's room and both of them started descending the stairs together. They looked into the large mirror on the opposite wall. Rajan's eyes were fully inebriated. Seeing him

Shadows: A Love Story

in that state, Rama's cheeks turned red and she started going downstairs quickly. On reaching the road, Rajan asked her–

'Were you at Lucknow before marriage?'

'No, at Delhi…'

'Oh, I feel as if I had seen you at Lucknow.'

'Not there, of course.'

'You must have liked Shimla, Rama Bhabi?'

'It seemed to be a nice place to start with but now it is losing its charm for me.'

Randhir had also descended the stairs by then. The three of them walked towards the Ridge via the Scandal Point. Rajan wanted to leave because it was dinner time and his companions were waiting for him in the Grand Hotel. Randhir invited him to dinner on Saturday. After the usual 'Good night', they wended their ways.

❑

Fifteen

When Rajan reached Craig Du on Saturday evening, he was wearing a dinner suit and a bow tie. There was a small folded hanky in his top coat pocket which had the fragrance of Evening-in-Paris. Randhir was drawing Goldflake puffs at that time in the drawing room. Rajan shook hands with Randhir after a long 'Hello……..' There was a big smile at play on their lips at that time.

'It is a very good place. An ideal location, indeed.'

'Yes, I got this lodge just by chance, otherwise it is very difficult to get a good place in Shimla.'

'Why are you trying to give an explanation? I won't ask you for such a suite for my own use. I am all right at the Grand Hotel.'

Rajan smiled and placed his cigarette in the ash tray. Rama was entering the room at that time. Rajan stood up and extended his hand towards her:

'Oh, I am sorry,' said he, folding his hands, 'Namaste, Bhabiji.'

'What was there in shaking hands?' said Randhir—'Do you think Rama is old-fashioned? She is quite modern.'

'There is no doubt, but she is rather reserved.'

'In fact, I am…' said Rama sitting on the arm of the sofa, 'interested in very few things. Though I am not taciturn by nature, I prefer to be alone.'

'It's too bad.'

Then commenting on her mental state, he said,

'A person living alone turns introvert and it is just possible that his or her view of life gets morbid.'

'I too have told her many a time,' said Randhir, 'One should mix up with others — man is a social animal.'

'The club does not leave him alone,' said Rama in a sort of romantic way–

'He comes from office and goes straightway to club and then he returns very late at night. I don't like that place at all — just go on gambling, smoking and drinking. ...Oh I am feeling a little upset.'

'You should take her out somewhere, Randhir– cinema or theatre.'

'My going to club is quite essential. As a matter of fact, the Chief Engineer and other officers come there and it is necessary for me to keep in touch with them; there are many things which need to be sorted out — our civilian life is something like this.'

After a little pause, Randhir said to Rajan,

'Rama does not stir out of the house. When she has a book in her hand, she forgets the world.'

'What are you reading these days, Rama Bhabi?'

'It's a novel...very interesting.'

'What is the name?'

'How green was my valley?'

'I too have heard a lot about this novel but I have not had the chance to read it so far. I had read *'For whom the bell tolls'* a few days back — you would also have read it, I believe.'

'Yes, I have read many of Hemingway's novels—a few days back I had seen the film based on his novel *'Snows of Climinjaro.'*

'You are interested in literature quite a lot. I read just to pass time.'

'Which writer do you like the most?'

'I have read Graham Greene quite a lot.'

After talking in this manner for some time, they came to the dining table. While taking their meals, Randhir and Rajan recalled the good old days when they were at Delhi's St. Stephens College. Rama heard them attentively. She liked the way Rajan could draw others towards himself through his suave manners - and it did not take them long to get close to each other.

❏

Sixteen

Rajan phoned up a few days later. He invited Rama to witness the staging of Oliver Goldsmith's play *'She stoops to conquer'* at Gaiety Theatre. In fact he had done the advance booking also. He asked Randhir also to accompany them but he could not go because of his preoccupations. He asked Rama to reach the Scandal Point at exact six. Rama hesitated in the beginning but she agreed after Rajan's repeated requests.

Rama wore a silk sari and blouse, had Max Factor wine-red lipstick and stepped into white sandals of her choice, which had sharp pointed heels. She found it a bit difficult to walk, with her high-heeled sandals, while going down the footpath but on reaching the wide road she walked in her normal gait. When she reached the Scandal Point, Rajan was there talking to a friend. As soon as he saw Rama, he shook hands with his friend and advanced towards her. She smiled and the dimple in her left cheek......They moved towards the Gaiety Theatre, which was just a two-minute walk from there. She looked at the theatre hall with keen interest. She had come there for the first time. A very large curtain of cherry-coloured velvet cloth had been hung at the stage. It was a small but very beautiful hall. There were boxes at the back of the hall and a gallery upstairs. The hall was getting filled. A boy was distributing pamphlets containing the brief story of the play and its cast. Rajan took a pamphlet and handed it over to Rama. Instead of reading it,

Rama started describing about the place of Goldsmith in literature and the importance of the play. Rajan heard her with rapt attention. While talking, she smiled once or twice and Rajan's eyes remained fixed on the dimple in her left cheek. He wished that she should continue smiling in that manner and he should keep on looking at her. A desire pulsated within him. He placed his arm at the back of Rama's chair. In this way, Rama's left shoulder came under Rajan's armpit. Rama felt a bit uneasy but she kept silent. Lights were switched off after some time and the curtain moved from the centre to the right and the left. The first scene had begun. Rama was taking keen interest and her eyes were fixed at the stage. Rajan's mind was not fully in the play. He furtively looked at the dimple on Rama's left cheek again and again. Rama, knowing that his eyes were at her face, looked at him. Noticing Rama looking at him, he turned his eyes towards the stage. They were sitting very close to the stage. The reflection of the strong lights, flashed at the stage, was falling on them also, which enabled them to look at each other properly. Rama felt more than once Rajan's warm breath on her left ear and neck. Although she was aware of all this and their closeness was getting closer, she did not want to be conscious of anything at that time.

The lights were switched on at the end of the first scene. The curtain returned to its place. People started talking among themselves. Rama and Rajan were tight-lipped. To lighten the burden of silence, Rama began to look at the people sitting in the galleries above. The people above were leaning at a low wall in front of them and looking at those sitting below. Rama looked back. The light was off in a box and a gem studded in someone's eardrop was shining– she turned her eyes away quickly.

They came out at the end of the play. In order to avoid the crowd, Rama positioned herself near the booking office window and Rajan went to the club to call Randhir. He returned quickly. Randhir was not there. Rama was surprised at his absence in the club. Where could he be at that time? She said nothing to Rajan about this. Both of them had two or three rounds of the Mall so that Randhir could meet them if he was there. It was going to be nine and it was dinner time. Rama wanted to go home but Rajan suggested that they should have another round or so. Turning from the Kwality Restaurant, Rajan suggested Rama for going up to Clarke's Hotel. He wanted to meet someone there for a few minutes. Rama agreed. She stood near the manager's office, and Rajan went upstairs. A waiter came to her and requested her to be seated in the drawing room next to the bar room. Rama was a bit tired. She followed the waiter. Only a man and a woman were sitting there. She could not trust her eyes. An Anglo-Indian woman was sitting with Randhir. She was smoking. Pegs of whisky were lying on the table before them. Rama was trying to recognize that woman but she was unable to recall where she had seen her. Randhir was flabbergasted to see her there. To hide his discomfiture, he stood up and said,

'Meet her. She is Miss Jones. She has come from Geneva to study Indian art. She is taking notes of paintings in the Arts Museum.'

Then pointing towards his wife, he said, 'She is my wife, Mrs. Rama Randhir.'

Rama greeted Miss Jones with folded hands and she responded with a smile and extended her hand towards her. Rama shook her hand and sat down on the sofa. She was still trying to recognize the woman. Getting up from the sofa, Miss Jones said, 'Excuse me, I am just coming.' Rama saw her going out. Then she recalled that evening in Davicos, when Rajan had met them for the first time.

❑

Seventeen

One day Rajan came to Craig Du in the evening. Randhir was not in at that time. Rama was playing with her daughter Nishi. On seeing Rajan, Rama said to her daughter, 'Say good evening to uncle.' Nishi cast a glance at Rajan and after saying 'good evening' clung to his legs. Rajan picked her up and took out of his pocket a packet of chocolate and handed it over to her. She took the packet and sat down on the carpet near the sofa and started removing its packing.

Rama and Rajan went into the balcony. English music was being aired at a distance. Rajan asked her:

'Rama Bhabi, you must be well-versed in ballroom dancing, I suppose.'

'No,' replied Rama.

'It's very strange — Randhir is a lover of ballroom dancing but you....'

'No, it's not so,' said Rama, interrupting him– 'In fact, I do not pay much attention to such things. I don't like all this.'

'What else you do not like, please tell me?' Rajan kept talking– 'It is the soul of modern society. I will tell Randhir to put you in some dance academy today itself.'

'No, I don't want it. I am Okay like this.'

'What do you mean?'

On hearing this, Rajan looked back and found Randhir coming:

'O, hello Randhir! You have come in good time. I was just cursing you.'

'Why this show of affection for me?'

'What's all this? Rama Bhabi doesn't know ball room dancing...'

'Just ask her. I have told her repeatedly but in vain. She does not like all these modern things.'

'If she does not like, you do like these. Don't you have even so much right over her?'

'I have already accepted my defeat. You can try.'

'Do you have records of dance music?'

'O, yes.'

'All right, bring in two or three and I will teach her right now how to raise her foot.'

Randhir went to the other room and brought back the record player. The tunes of Samba and Waltz echoed in the air for some time. Rajan placed his left hand at Rama's waist and holding her left hand in his right hand raised it to her shoulder level. Rama's other hand was on Rajan's shoulder. The record was playing. Rajan's eyes were at Rama's feet and he taught her how to raise her foot to the tune of music. The records were played three or four times. Rama gained self-confidence. She was raising her foot like Rajan's without any hesitation. Rajan's fingers were dug into Rama's waist and he turned her to the right or left as he desired. This continued for twenty to twenty five minutes. Then this lesson was practised daily for half an hour or so. Rama had learnt all the dance moves. She had imagined that the dance would be difficult to learn but it was not so in reality. While teaching her, Rajan sometimes joined her to his chest and tightened the clasp and then stepped back a little. There was nothing new for Rama about Rajan's mannerism. In fact, sometimes she even warmed up to him when he made such moves.   ❑

Eighteen

Dinner-dance was on at Davicos. Rama and Rajan were at one table. A cocktail peg was lying before Rajan and Rama was drinking sherry. They were absorbed in talking. Orchestra stopped for a while. Some couples came up to the dance floor. Orchestra had resumed its play and the feet were being raised slowly. Rajan had a long draught of his drink and while looking at Rama, he pointed towards her glass. Rama took the glass in her hand and started having small sips. After that they stood up and joined the dancing couples. Orchestra continued tunefully for fifteen to twenty minutes. Then the tone was at a high pitch and the beat quickened and the dance-steps changed. The couples separated and danced independently. They swirled on their feet again and again and clapped their hands at intervals. Their feet were rising to the tune of music. It appeared as if electric current were passing through their veins. Rama and Rajan were dancing blissfully. Pink lines had been drawn in Rama's eyes. Her body appeared to be a conflagration from top to toe. Her blouse had got raised up. When she raised her hands to clap, her dark armpits were exposed. After some time the orchestra changed its tune and again the earlier tune was played— gradually the feet were seen rising normally, the hands being placed on the waists, the whispering and

Shadows: A Love Story

occasional reaction of striking against one another in the crowd. The orchestra stopped suddenly and all of them returned to their tables.

While sitting in the chair, Rama heaved a sigh of relief and wiped perspiration off her forehead with her hanky. Rajan pressed Rama's foot lightly with the tip of his shoe. She smiled and the dimple in her left cheek…..

Rajan ordered the bearer to bring a large peg of Johny Walker for him and sherry for Rama. She did not want to drink more but Rajan was able to persuade her. Such an evening was a rarity in Rama's life. She was not in a position to think clearly at that time. She only knew that they were sitting in the Davicos, the orchestra was being played and the chords of her body were throbbing. Rajan gulped down half the peg of whisky in one go and his eyes started looking for the dimple in her left cheek. Lights were switched off suddenly—only dim lights of many colours were focused at the dance floor. Orchestra was resumed. Two English girls came out of a dark corner to the dance floor and started doing cabaret dance. This was a special item of the programme and somewhat new for the people of Shimla. Their legs were bare up to their thighs. After some time they removed their bush-shirts also…they started doing rock 'N' roll in the multi-colour lights. Then holding their sandals and bush-shirts in their hands, they ascended the stairs leading to the upper room. Lights were switched on in the hall. But for long the same bodies continued dancing before their eyes…..the white and bare bodies…

Rama and Rajan descended the stairs of Davicos at eleven forty five. Rama's feet were shaky on the ground. Rajan encircled her waist with his arm. Taking small steps, they walked towards Craig Du. When they left the road and started walking up the footpath, Rajan squeezed Rama in his arms. It was pitch dark on the footpath at that time. The moonshine was sieving through the leaves of the trees on both sides. There was complete silence everywhere. A bird's chirping at a distance thickened the darkness. Rajan laid Rama on the ground on pine straws. His burning lips, passing through the dimple in her left cheek, rested on her throbbing lips and from the lips again to the hollow in her left cheek.

❑

Nineteen

Rama woke up at 7 in the morning the next day. She stretched herself fully and smiled. Randhir was returning the same evening after a week's tour. A thought rose in a corner of her mind and slowly got over her emotions. She changed her dress quickly and started descending the footpath. As she was walking down, her glance rested at the hanky lying under a tree. It was Rajan's hanky. She took her lower lip between her teeth and kicked off the hanky into the gorge. Her heart began to thump. She looked back and then started walking down the path.

She went straightway to Grand Hotel. Rajan was surprised to see her there but he looked at her and smiled. Rama told him that she had come out for a walk and just turned this side. They talked for some time. Then Rajan encircled her with his arms and pulled her towards himself. Like a ripe fruit, she fell on his chest.

On reaching home, she dropped herself into bed and cried for quite some time. She wanted to shut her eyes for the death to be quick in putting a seal on them. She was unable to bear this pain. She was reminded again and again of Naresh's letter in which he had written about the ideal one cherishes. She felt a desire to read that letter again. She got up and brought the letter out of her suitcase. As she started reading, she realized her mistake. She had in fact brought out her own letter which she had written to Naresh from the Naino's drawing room but had forgotten to post the same. It was also lying with Naresh's letter. She opened it and started reading:

'Dear Naresh,

Sometimes I think there may hardly be a person in the world who has been able to attain his ideal. In fact attaining the ideal is not only difficult, but impossible too. When we are able to have a glimpse of our ideal somewhere, we feel somewhat satisfied. But if one does not even have a glimpse, one's life becomes a bed of thorns, and what else? In such a state of mind, one tries to find a reflection of one's ideal elsewhere but this is not easy. This is a slippery path and one wavers at every step. A little carelessness, and the crystal of life slips out of hand and is broken into pieces. I am confident of myself that the crystal of my life will never slip out of my hand and break into pieces. I would not even let a crack develop in it.'

After reading the letter, Rama wiped her eyes with the corner of her scarf and kept gazing at the opposite wall for some time. She felt a creeping sensation within her. She tore off the letter into small pieces and flung it out of the balcony. Nishi was playing below. Looking at so many bits of paper flying in the air, she felt very happy and said, clapping her hands:

'Throw off some more confetti, mom.'

❑

Twenty

Rama's life was now passing through a very strange phase. Conflict was growing in her mind. What she had hated most was overpowering her. She never loved Rajan. Rather she hated him to the utmost. When he was not before her, she considered herself quite clean, pure and very light but his closeness made her lose her wits and she failed to control her emotions. Rajan was aware of her weakness.

One day Rama went to the Mall for shopping. Rajan met her on the way back. He smiled and she too could not restrain her smile. They walked side by side for some time. Then Rajan asked her–

'How are you?'

'Fine.'

'Seem to have done a lot of shopping.'

'No….not much.'

'How is Randhir?'

'O.K.'

'Has not met me for many days.'

She kept quiet.

'Let's sit somewhere for some time.'

'I'm in a hurry. Will be delayed.'

'Why be in such a hurry? It's not even six.'

Rama could say nothing.

'We will go up to St. Bedes — it is very nice walking that side.'

After reaching St. Bedes's crossing, they started going up the footpath on the left which led to an old building of the Convent. That building had been destroyed in fire many years ago and only four walls stood there as its ruins and there were heaps of rubble everywhere. Of course, the building had reached the crumbling stage. Its beauty could, however, be imagined even now. Roses, cosmos and dahlias were still blooming in narrow-beds. Pine, and other hill trees were swinging in the air with the same majesty. There was a freshness and crispness in the atmosphere.

Rama and Rajan sat down on a rock. Rama's brain was tightly held in a grip. She wanted to say something but could not. When Rajan was with her, something gripped her brain in its claw and her sanity parted company with her.

'Rama….!' said Rajan in a low tone.

She raised her eyes and looked at him. Observing a combination of emotions, desire and pleading in his eyes, her heart pounded violently. She was always frightened on seeing Rajan in this condition– she did not fear him, but herself, her own weakness.

Rajan had aroused Rama's passion by igniting something within her. He had taken her fully under his control. She regarded Rajan a wild animal who was fully aware of the weaknesses of the female gender, but unable to gauge the subtlety of feminine emotions— rather he had never risen so high as to probe her sensibilities:

'Rama, I have a grievance….Rama dear.'

'Against me?'

'Yes. I have been feeling for some time that your touch no longer has the same warmth. When I have your body in my arms, your mind is miles away from me….'

Shadows: A Love Story

'I am the same... as before. I don't know what makes you think so?'

'Rama...' Rajan held her hand...

'I love you deeply, limitless love it is.'

Rama kept quiet and he continued,

'Do you also love me the same way, Rama?'

He raised her chin with two of his fingers and asked her...

Rama stood up without giving a reply. Then she moved from there to stand against the wall of the crumbled building. There was a brazier of red tiles and close to it was a small ramp of cement. She seated herself on the ramp and joined her back to the wall. She felt like crying to her fill, not in little sobs but very loudly. She wanted to shriek and wail, so very loudly that the voice of her soul would be buried under her shrieks. But she did not cry. Crying would have meant her defeat. She did not want to be humiliated. Her being was getting torn into shreds. Mental knots were being formed in her thoughts and the pain in her heart was increasing.

'These black locks, this fair face....' said Rajan raising up her lock of hair fallen on her left cheek. He placed his lips on the short curly hair covering her neck. Rama felt a strong tremor in her body. She felt as if she were shrinking and had turned into a dot. The dot began to dance before her eyes– a savage dance. She shut her eyes for a moment. Suddenly a hand turned into a snake and moved sideways over her, its venom permeated every pour of her body and her limbs became listless. She felt something sticking in her throat. She opened her eyes with a start. The same dot was dancing before her eyes, doing the same savage dance. The dot, as it was dancing, rose up and entered the beak of a bird perched on the yonder tree. The bird began to strike its beak against the branch of the tree, once, twice, thrice.... It was continuously striking its beak against the tree. Rama again shut her eyes. Three, four five…Some ticking sound was coming to her ears. The sea waves were striking against her body and going back. A lamp got lit, its flame got into an ecstasy…right, left, left, right — the flame had got into a stupor, and with its light had been lit countless lamps in rain-drops fallen on the grass. The entire atmosphere seemed to be ablaze. Rama opened her eyes. The dot stuck into the beak of the bird was also burning. Rama's eyes got wet and the bird got out of sight, but its beak continued to be seen. The beak was striking against the branch, and then the dot dropped out of the beak, but before falling on the ground, a strong wave washed it away — and over-shadowed the existence of the burning bird.

❏

Shadows: A Love Story

Twenty-one

Rama remained at Shimla that year during winter. Winter sports were being organized in Kufri in the second week of February. She was very much fond of watching skiing. That day Rajan came towards Craig Du with his jeep at 10 in the morning and reached the cart road close by. Rama and Randhir were already waiting for him. Passing through Sanjauli, they reached Dhalli. They bought a bottle of Black Knight whisky from there. There was a heavy traffic of jeeps, cars and buses beyond Dhalli and the number of those going on foot was no less. Heaps of snow were lying on both sides of the road. There was a great hustle and bustle on the stretch from Dhalli to Kufri. He stopped his jeep a little short of Kufri bazaar and they had coffee in the Himachal Winter Sports Club. After stopping there for about fifteen minutes they started going uphill beyond Kufri bazaar. The hill was covered with snow. Skiing was on at the mountain peak. There was the layer of three to four feet of snow turned into ice under their feet. People were walking up very carefully, with the support of sticks. Though Randhir had held Rama's arm, she was slipping almost at every step. Once or twice she escaped falling down when Rajan held her hand. Rama slipped at a spot in such a way that both of them could not control her. Rather they themselves slipped and went rolling back quite a lot:

'Hope the bottle is safe,' Rajan asked Randhir.

'See how much worried are you about the bottle? Unmindful of some sort of a fracture,' said Rama shaking snow off her clothes.

When they reached the peak they were panting for breath. People were taking tea, sitting on the floor of snow turned ice or taking lunch. Rajan spread his overcoat on the ice and all of them sat down on it. From the hill in front of them, ten to fifteen men and women, with wooden skis tied to their feet and holding sticks in their hands, were gliding down the slope quickly. It seemed as if they were flying in the air. Sometimes one fell down and the sticks were thrown away and he reached the starting point sliding downhill. There were individual players who showed their prowess in the game and then started the collective race down the slope.

Randhir and Rajan kept drinking whisky with snow thrown into it, while Rama kept on smiling, sitting beside them. It was the smile bathed in the colourfulness of the wonderful time. Rajan took off his coat and lying down on the ice, started sliding downward. Randhir also followed him holding the bottle in his hand. Rama kept standing there. When Randhir reached close to Rajan, they had a few more draughts of whisky. Randhir kept lying there. But Rajan went up the ascent and reached where Rama was standing. In black jeans, white pullover and printed scarf Rama looked a dashing beauty. Rajan held her arm and rushed down the slope. They ran for some time, then they fell down on the ice deliberately and rolling down reached where Randhir was lying in deep snow.

It was four in the evening when they came down the skiing hill. Kufri bazaar was over-crowded. They took lot of time passing through it. Water had frozen in a big tank near the bus stop. Some people were walking on the ice slab and slipping

Shadows: A Love Story

down. Those going on foot pelted snow-balls on their jeep. Rajan was driving. Rama and Randhir sat close to him. When the ball hit them, it broke into small bits in a moment. They stopped the jeep and filled some snow in it to make counter-attacks on the way. When they reached home, Rajan and Randhir were very much tired, but wild rose was blooming in Rama's cheeks.

They had their evening tea sitting in the balcony of Craig Du. They felt fresh after taking tea. When evening got darker, Randhir and Rajan uncorked another bottle of whisky. Rajan asked Rama also to take a peg but she declined. After some time, when Randhir also compelled her to take a small peg to avoid catching cold, she could not say 'no'. The warmth of whisky brought a glint in her eyes and the dimple on her left cheek deepened further. Rajan looked intently at her and poured another peg of whisky into her glass. Rajan clinked his glass with Randhir's– "To your health and happiness"– said Rajan and Randhir said, 'The same to you.' Then he clinked his glass with Rama's.

'To our happy married life'….said Randhir.

Rama said nothing in reply. Something flashed in her eyes and vanished instantly. She looked at Rajan but his eyes were fixed at his glass. Rama looked into space out of the window. Lost in her thoughts, she kept sitting there for some time.

When they sat at the dinner table, there was complete silence. Except for the clanking of glasses and plates, there was no other sound in the room. After dinner, they sat down in the drawing room and listened to music over the radiogram. Both of them were dead drunk but Rama's condition was somewhat different. The chords of her body were vibrating. Whirlpools were being formed in her thoughts. Her sentience had started dozing.

When Rajan rose up to leave, Randhir stopped him. It was very late at night and the road was full of snow. It was not safe to go out at that time. Rama took no interest in his going or not going and went into the bedroom. Randhir had Rajan's bed laid on the sofa in the drawing room.

Rama woke up at six in the morning. She wrapped around herself the gown, lying near the sofa in the drawing room, and on opening the door, she went into the bedroom. Randhir was fast asleep. She took off the gown and put on her clothes lying on the carpet. Suddenly, Randhir's words–

'To our happy married life'

echoed in her ears and she kept on staring at Randhir's face, while sitting at the edge of the bed.

❑

Twenty-two

Those were the last days of March. It had been raining for the last two days. When the rain stopped for some time, the sun rose. The mist began to rise above the foothill. The mist spread all round in no time and it started raining again. Rama, sitting in the balcony, was looking at the mist spreading over the yonder hill when someone placed his hand on her shoulder. Startled, she looked back. Rajan was smiling.

'Scared?'

'Oh, no.'

'I am going out tomorrow for a week. I thought I should meet you before going.'

'You had made no mention of this day before yesterday in the evening.'

'I have received the orders today only. There is some urgent work. I am going to New Delhi.'

'All right, be seated. Shall I call for tea?'

'No harm.'

Rama turned back to ask for tea. Rajan went into the drawing room. He removed his coat and placed it on the back of a chair. Rama continued to look at the clouds gathering and dispersing as she stood in the balcony. Loosening the knot of his tie, Rajan again came out to the balcony and stood behind her–

'What are you looking at?'

'Nothing'

'Still.'

'I am watching that mist. Just now there was sunshine on that hill. Then mist rose up from the gorge and it overshadowed the hill in no time. I am thinking that this hill, even if it tried to get out of the mist, could not.'

'What is the need of its getting out of the mist? The mist would disperse itself, in a little while.'

'But when?'

Rama asked him raising her voice at a high pitch. Rajan was surprised at her tone and holding her arm he came back to the drawing room.

Tea was lying on the tripod there. He took the cup of tea from Rama's hand and pressed her hand a little. She smiled impulsively. Rajan's eyes dug into the hollow in her left cheek and he went on sliding deep into the pitfall.

'Take your tea, it's getting cold.' She reminded him.

Rajan placed the cup on the tripod and moved behind Rama's chair. He raised Rama's face up with his cupped hands, bent down a little and tried to kiss her...Suddenly the door opened and Randhir came in. Rajan stepped back instantly. Rama tried to stand up when her foot hit the tripod and the cup of tea fell down. The long line of spilt tea got absorbed slowly into the carpet.

❑

Shadows: A Love Story

Twenty-three

Rajan had returned from tour but had not gone to Craig Du to see them. Randhir had said nothing to him that day but Rajan had read something in his eyes. He did not want to confront Randhir. He had tried to ask Rama many a time about that day's incident but he could not muster enough courage for that. He was remembering again and again the evening when Rama had suddenly come into the drawing room of the Clarke's hotel and he had introduced her to his keep in a make believe manner.

One day Rama was sitting in the lawn knitting Nishi's socks and enjoying the warmth of sunshine. Her face exuded an equipoise. She was happy that although the hill could not move from its place, the mist had scattered on its own. She turned her neck a little to look towards that hill. She smiled and started knitting again.

'Your telephone, madam.' Called the servant from inside. Keeping the knitting pins and wool on the chair and adjusting the loose end of her sari, Rama went in–

'Hello!'

'Who, Rama? I am Rajan.'

'Yes?'

'How are you? It's many days since we met last….'

'I hardly get any time from household chores. I seldom go to the Mall.'

'But when can we…..?

'………' Rama kept quiet.

'I am sure you would meet me at the Red Cross Fair tomorrow?'

'I don't think so.'

'On my transfer, I am leaving Shimla after about a week.....what's the harm in meeting me before I leave….'

Rama felt herself weak at her knees. She was finding it difficult to keep on standing there. Before replacing the receiver, she blurted out, 'Not tomorrow….some other……'

The receiver dropped out of her hand and she got dug into the sofa.

Next day a conflict started in her mind. Should she go to the Red Cross Fair or not? Before Rajan had phoned, the boat of her emotions was floating smoothly. But now she found herself caught into a whirlpool which was drawing her down deeper and still deeper. Ultimately she decided not to go to the Red Cross Fair at any cost.

Her restlessness increased further the next day. It became difficult for her to spend the day sitting at home alone. She lay in bed till one o'clock and then suddenly something struck her mind. She started getting ready. She wore olive green sari, tucked a bright red rose in her hairbun, stepped into her pointed high-heel sandals and walked towards the Mall.

When she reached the Scandal Point, the clock at the General Post Office struck two. There was still half an hour or so for the matinee show to start. To while away the time, she moved towards the Grand Hotel. Walking in the sun, she found the welcome warmth. She was very happy because she had overcome her weakness with a determined effort. This weakness was that of the hill which could not defend herself against the onslaught of mist. Lost in her thoughts, she moved beyond Grand Hotel and then returned. As she was about to reach the Telegraph Office, she saw Rajan coming up the narrow path. He was looking at her–

'I knew you would certainly meet me….'

'At least this time your thinking is certainly wrong.'

'In what way?'

'I have not come to go to the Red Cross Fair, but to watch the matinee show.

'All right, I will accompany you to the matinee show. I have no special interest in the Fair.'

'No, you will…..' She stopped. She knew Rajan quite well. She considered it wiser to go to the Red Cross Fair than to the matinee show.

'All right. We will go to the Red Cross Fair.'

'As you like,' said Rajan leaning his neck to one side.

Both of them went to the Wind Cliff side. Red Cross Fair was held in the ground of the residence of the Lt. Governor of Himachal Pradesh. Stalls had been set up along the flower-beds and women and girls stood at the stalls. Rajan was in a great mood. He was losing a rupee or two at every stall. They lingered quite a lot at one stall. There were many people in front of that stall. Firstly it was a new game and secondly the girl at the stall was very smart. A chart was lying at the table. Four small plastic horses stood at the starting point— one was named 'my love', the second one was 'thunder', the third was 'heart' and the fourth, 'arrow'. The girl at the stall held the dice in her hand. Whosoever wanted to play the game had to place a rupee at the similar horse printed on the chart and the game started with four rupees. The girl cast the dice at the chart and the horse of the player went as many steps ahead as had been indicated on the chart. Then came the turn of the second player and his horse also moved ahead according to the points won by him. The horse which reached the destination first of all, was given a chocolate packet.

Rama took a lot of interest in this game. Her face had got tense on seeing Rajan but now she was feeling quite relaxed and happy. Rama put her stake always at the horse named 'heart' and Rajan at the 'arrow.' Rama lost first two rounds but her horse won the last round. She clapped like a child.

Then they moved ahead of that stall. Rama and Rajan drew lottery tickets as they went ahead. The lottery was to be opened after the sale of about one hundred tickets and the winner was to be given a large cake. They sat at the tea stall for some time and then they moved towards the hall. Many people had assembled in the hall. The prize cake was lying at a table. A little girl drew the lot. As the slip was being unfolded, people looked at the girl with baited breaths and then the number was announced. Rama read the number on her ticket….she had won the lottery. Passing through the crowd, Rama went to the stage and brought back the cake—clappings resounded in the hall.

'You are very lucky,' said Rajan going with her towards the door.

'You had bought the ticket,' replied Rama.

'But it was in your name!' said he taking her hand into his own.

'It is getting cold. We should go back,' Rama felt a chill as she said this.

'Why haven't you brought your coat?'

'I had to go back after the cinema show, but now it is so very late.'

Both of them started descending the footpath which joined a dust road. The dust road went round the Wind Cliff hill and ended in the Chaura Maidan. Rama did not want to go that way. But as Rajan insisted that it was a short cut, she agreed. They ate chocolate going along the dust road and gossiped. Taking a turn they stopped — the sun was setting and it had spread its crimson hue across the sky. Rama almost got lost in the spectacle and occupied the bench lying nearby. Suddenly she was wistful. She wanted to be the part of that environment. The ball of the sun was vanishing at the horizon. Then it slid down and there was darkness all round.

'It is getting dark and there is no light on the road,' said Rama picking up the cake box.

'We have come very close to the Chaura Maidan now. We will go there after a while.'

Rajan took the cake box from Rama's hand and kept it aside. Then he got closer to Rama. She felt a bit uneasy and left her seat. Rajan pulled her towards him and tried to kiss her. Rama did her best to wriggle out of his hold but the clasp was too tight. Rajan's eyeballs dilated and he began to heave noisily. She put her hands on his chest and tried to push him away but he further leaned on her. Rama fixed her foot on the iron arm of the bench and tried to get up with a jerk. But her head struck against the other iron arm and she fainted.

Rajan loosened his grip and looked around. It had become quite dark. The road was deserted. He adjusted Rama's clothes properly and carried her in his arms to the Chaura Maidan. Then he set her in a rickshaw and sprinkled water on her face. She regained consciousness shortly afterwards. She got unnerved as she saw some people surrounding the rickshaw. Then in a sort of delirium she fixed her eyes at Rajan's face. He apologized in a low tone. Tears welled up in Rama's eyes on hearing his voice. Placing her hands on her face she began to cry bitterly.

❑

Twenty Four

Rama changed her clothes on reaching home and lay in bed. Randhir had not yet returned from the club. Her head was pounding with pain. She gazed at the ceiling as she lay totally fatigued. Tears kept flowing down the corners of her eyes. Then she felt as if she were being crushed under a very heavy load. Her eyelids joined together slowly and she fainted.

Randhir returned at 11 o'clock. He was drunk as usual. When the servant sought his permission to lay the table for dinner, he was rebuked. Finding his master in such a mood, he did not have the courage to tell him that the madam was unwell and had not taken her dinner. Randhir changed his clothes hurriedly and lay down in bed. His fingers got entangled in Rama's hair and his weight became unbearable for her. Rama tried to push him away with both the hands, but her arms had lost all energy.

Randhir turned his back on Rama after some time and went to sleep. She was in a strange condition that night. Her brain was like a station through which an electric train passed making a hissing sound and soon after the passing of the earlier train, another train came in hissing. Pinpricks were tormenting her, her temples were burning hot and every pour of her body was scorching her. She pushed aside the quilt, switched on

Shadows: A Love Story

the table lamp and took a draught of water out of the golden glass pitcher lying on the tripod. Her heart was pounding. She got up, opened the door slowly and went out.

There was moonlight in the lawn. Cool breeze was lifting the veils off jasmine buds. There was a sort of intoxication in the atmosphere, as if a spell had been cast over it. She stepped out barefoot and walked on the grass covered with dew, her soles absorbed the coolness of the earth. Gradually, she regained her equipoise, her feelings threaded into a chain. Her eyes got drenched in tears which flowed down her cheeks and then fell on the grass— perhaps the dew was getting its debt repaid.

SELF HELP

Management Guru
LORD KRishNA

Tips for achieving

Paritranaya Sadhunaam

Vinashaya Cha Dushkritaam

Dharmasansthapanaarthaya
Sambhavaami Yuge Yuge

O.P.Jha

No Dream Too Big
BELIEVE IN DETERMINATION

Joginder Singh

DYNAMIC MEMORY
SURE SUCCESS IN INTERVIEWS

Tarun Chakarborty

DYNAMIC MEMORY
GROUP DISCUSSION

Tarun Chakraborty

Time Management

- Achieve a better control on time and climb the ladder of success
- Acquire unmatched time manauvering skills
- Learn how to detail when you run out of time
- Meet all the deadlines without panic

Dr. Rekha Vyas

108 INCOME-TAX MANTRAS FOR TAX SAVING

Subhash Lakhotia

TIPS OF PROPERTY

Buying, Selling, Renting & Tax Planning

R.N. LAKHOTIA SUBHASH LAKHOTIA

SUBHASH LAKHOTIA
TAX GURU

HOW TO BECOME A MILLIONAIRE

Practical Money Making Ideas
for Complete Financial Freedom

ASHU DUTT
Market Guru and Bestselling Author

MASTER THE STOCK MARKET

Jolly Uncle

Stories that Enlighten You

JPS Jolly

DARE TO DREAM DARE TO EXCEL

- Never give up
- Make your own destiny
- Determination is the key to success
- The power inherent in the unfailing spirit

Dr. Harikrishna Devsare

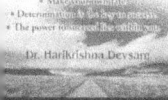

HEAL-PILL
Incurable ⇄ Cure within

Dr. Biswaroop Roy Chowdhury

108 INVESTMENT MANTRAS

Time Tested
Tips
For Beneficial
Investment

Badminton Queen of India
Saina Nehwal

⊙ **DIAMOND BOOKS** X-30, Okhla Industrial Area, Phase-II New Delhi-110020
Tel : 91+11-40712200, email : sales@dpb.in   Shop online at www.diamondbook.in